A Mixed Bag

Agnes McIntyre

 FriesenPress

One Printers Way
Altona, MB R0G 0B0
Canada

www.friesenpress.com

ISBN
978-1-03-830399-8 (Hardcover)
978-1-03-830398-1 (Paperback)
978-1-03-830400-1 (eBook)

1. FICTION, SHORT STORIES (SINGLE AUTHOR)

Distributed to the trade by The Ingram Book Company

Dedication

To my children Gary, Grant, Colleen . . . with deepest love.
Ever humbled by the privilege of being your mom . . .

. . . Michael and Daniel . . .

. . . my blessed grandchildren . . . Riley, Nathan, Winston . . .

. . . mention must also be made of the pets who have influenced my
life and writing by their unwavering capacity for love and loyalty
. . . Fuzi, Jonathan, Polo, Ellie . . . whose sheer presence
brought riches beyond measure . . . and now, Mitzi, for continuing
the legacy . . .

♥ ♥ ♥

Table of Contents

The Gift

THE PAPER WAS GARISH. HARSH. Cartoonish even. Totally ill-suited for Happy Anniversary wrapping.

It's perfect, I thought triumphantly. And yet…I found myself hesitating, suddenly wondering if I should follow through with my plan. *It's stupid*, I told myself. *Plain childish*. By the time the near ghoulish paper was adorned with an elaborate gold ribbon, I had made up my mind.

"I'm doing it," I muttered aloud to no one in particular, unless you counted my dozing pug, Dixie. Other than a brief twitch of her ears, she exhibited no interest whatsoever at my presence.

Scrutinizing the new dress and jacket in the full-length closet mirror, I sighed. It was as good as it was going to get. Picking up my clutch and the gift, I snatched the keys from their basket and hurried out the door.

On the way, I impulsively decided to make an unscheduled, last-minute detour. It was a few miles outside of my route, but today's occasion marked a good excuse for another look-see at the Sweet Escapes Motel. Rounding the corner of the street, I was stunned by what I saw. It was gone!

The last time I'd been here, the dilapidated structure under its faded sign had still been standing. Well, actually, "leaning" would be more accurate. Still, in the space of several months, it had literally disappeared! In its place now stood a tidy, dull-looking, single-story strip mall. Though a couple of vacant store fronts sported 'For Lease' signs, I couldn't help but smile at the three businesses already in place: Jeb's Liquor Emporium, Bert's Cannabis Haven, and Lil's Love Shop. *Well,* I thought, shaking my head, *all of them* do *fit in with the general theme 'Sweet Escapes' always promoted!* This was just a more current version.

Musing on this turn of events, I turned my car around and proceeded to "The Manor." As the gated mansion came into view, I had to admit that it definitely lived up to its majestic billing. Georgian columns, luscious shrubbery, and Victorian atmosphere was shielded gracefully by the ornate wrought-iron fencing surrounding the property. A couple of eager young attendants in white shirts and black suits were on site, directing traffic within a parking lot already nearly full. It seemed no expense had been spared for this celebration. Somehow, that didn't surprise me. Adelaide had always had luxurious tastes. Even way back when.

She's obviously made good, I brooded silently for a moment before admonishing myself sternly: *Is that jealousy, Isabella? Stay focused.*

*   *   *

AFTER PARKING WHERE DIRECTED, I sauntered towards the grand hall. There are times when I still try to convince myself that I look younger than my seventies. This was not one of those days. I wanted to blend in and did so easily, joining the fragmented line of (mostly) septuagenarians heading towards the entrance. It was then that I noticed invitations were being checked at the door. *Damn.* I had hoped to avoid a screening for this "Invitation Only" event, an evasion due exclusively to the fact that I hadn't been invited.

Somewhat tacky to check, I thought, as I considered what lay ahead. It's sometimes difficult to anticipate at which point a situation might go awry, so it's always handy to formulate some type of backup plan.

Since I had no choice but to accept looking like a senior, I liked to play that card, peddling my elder status for all it was worth. As such, it can be extremely beneficial to bolster my grey hair and wrinkles with the addition of fumbling confusion, which is very effective during interactions with the young. Simply put, they don't know what to do. Generally speaking, they prefer to take the easy route and just wave me through.

Glancing around, I spied a visibly agitated couple a short distance ahead and quickly decided that they would do nicely. Managing to squeeze myself immediately behind them, it was time to implement Plan B.

"Albert," admonished a grey-coiffed lady in a chic black coat, "what do you mean you don't have the invitation?"

"I-I thought you had it," he stammered, in obvious embarrassment. "You always look after that sort of thing, Maria."

"It's okay," chirped the cheery-voiced greeter. If she was thinking that old people were *such a pain,* her attitude was carefully concealed behind the façade of a huge, fawning smile.

"Oh my," I interrupted, allowing a worried expression to overtake my features. "I'm sorry to say that I have the same problem. In fact, I think I may have left it in my other purse."

"It really is totally alright," continued the chirper, waving her hand towards the doorway. "Go right on in. It's open seating, so please make yourselves comfortable wherever you like."

I retracted my original cynicism about her attitude. Her pleasant demeanour seemed truly genuine. My guess was that the young woman had already made a general assumption that the elderly didn't crash parties and would *definitively* never stir from their homes just to attend useless events to which they weren't invited. She had much to learn! In time, she would no doubt come to understand that many lonely and/or underappreciated oldsters would happily do exactly that. Blend, mingle, and enjoy—all while receiving a delicious free meal!

Retaining my glued smile while repeatedly mumbling thanks, I eventually made it indoors. Once there, I swiftly detached myself from the duo while simultaneously ditching my muddled manner.

My eyes swept the room. No expense had been spared in rehashing the happy nuptials fifty years earlier. Lavish decorations festooned the tables and walls, including a gigantic banner that read, "Happy 50th Stuart and Adelaide!" Several side tabletops had been loaded down with delectable pastries and edible concoctions, and there was another table, attended by a couple of bored teenagers—granddaughters, I assumed—where guests were expected to sign in.

I hadn't planned on signing the register but suddenly couldn't resist. Adopting an entirely illegible signature, I added a cryptic comment that abruptly popped into my thoughts, and then smiled, wondering what Adelaide would make of it: "You both have always deserved each other." I then hastily slipped away before anyone could put together the words with their author.

There were at least twenty tables, each set with ten place settings. *Who really knows two hundred people to invite to anything?* I pondered. I could barely come up with a dozen.

Jealous, are we?

Shut up, I admonished my inner voice.

Yes, Adelaide would have certainly spent the last fifty years carefully accumulating acquaintances (if not friends) of a particular refinement. Well-read and monied, naturally.

I instantly located the gift table, wondering vaguely if the invite had stipulated "No gifts," as most do these days. Of course, even if it had, I had learned long ago that people generally ignore this sentiment. On the rare occasion where I'd actually paid proper attention to such stipulations, I usually found myself the odd man out. Most everyone seems compelled to bring *something*. With the slightest of hesitations, I added my ribboned package to the base of the small mountain of gifts already assembled.

Selecting a table to sit at was a learned skillset. Over the course of many years, I'd attended enough weddings and celebrations alone to ascertain easily what seats to avoid and which to gravitate towards, depending entirely on what type of conversation I wanted to be a part of.

Today was a bit different. I wanted to engage in as little chatting as possible. I wasn't there to interact. Only to observe. I stood around at the back for a bit, ultimately shifting myself about the room as though fully absorbed in studying all of the tasty delights on offer. Eventually, I halted at the cocktail bar, considering which potion to order from the young bartender. *He looks about fourteen,* I thought grumpily. Generally, I accepted the fact that the older I got, the younger the kids looked. Occasionally, though, I still found myself taken aback.

I experienced a sudden and unexpected awkward moment when I realized that it was at least forty years since I'd had any contact with either "the bride" or "the groom," and I was hit with a momentary urge to flee. And to do so quickly! It all felt so wrong. *What am I doing?* It took a moment more to quash the fearful spasm rumbling around my innards. I felt out of sync and attributed it to the visible wealth on display all around me. The entire atmosphere breathed opulence.

More to keep my hands busy than anything else, I finally ordered a ginger ale on ice. Twirling the glass slightly, I stayed in the back of the room, recognizing the odd face here and there—not that they looked even remotely like anyone I remembered. This event wasn't unlike a school reunion. I never really managed to identify anyone definitively from their looks. Mostly, just like at such a reunion, I simply envisioned who would be most likely to attend, and then went from there. It worked here too. Luckily, no one acknowledged me. I looked very different from the young woman they would have known at one time, and more importantly, they certainly wouldn't have expected me to attend! I felt like everyone was aware I was an imposter. An intruder. In reality, not being recognized or noticed at all felt infinitely worse.

The tables were filling up nicely, and eventually, the Master of Ceremonies stepped up to a small podium. I deduced that this had to be Adelaide's brother, Peter, who was still sporting the same hawkish nose and thin features.

"Ladies and gentlemen," he began, his voice straining to be heard over the loud chatter of those assembled and their clinking glassware. "Can everyone please take their seats?"

I slipped effortlessly into a vacant chair at a table conveniently close to an exit, settling my clutch on the table before me. Looking at my tablemates, I offered them a practiced, muted smile. There were four couples already seated, and a moment later, a woman slipped into the only other vacant seat, right beside me. Abruptly realizing my poor choice in seat selection, I knew that it was too late to make a change.

A sparkling smile lit the woman's face at seeing another single table-mate right beside her. Blessedly, she resembled no one I could recall. She opened her mouth to speak just as the microphone at the front of the room again screeched to life. Offering her a vacant, noncommittal smile, I turned away quickly, simulating a rapt attentiveness to the activities at the front of the room and thinking, *Damn, damn, damn!*

"Ladies and gentlemen," the voice on the microphone said again in a slow droning voice. "Our family is very happy to see so many of you able to join in the celebration of Stuart and Adelaide's fiftieth!" He started clapping then, and after giving a roving nod to the crowd before him, a round of generous applause followed.

My hands remained in my lap. *Definitely Peter*, I reasoned. *Still sounds like the sniveling loser he was back then.*

Adelaide stood first, nodding and smiling a stretched, plastic-looking smile that revealed perhaps one surgery too many. I chortled silently. With one bony hand, she prodded a rather reluctant Stuart up to his feet. *Still the subservient shadow*, I thought, snorting inwardly. *Albeit a shrunken shadow,* I reassessed, as a sudden sympathetic twinge fought for space among my tangled thoughts.

"Still a puppet, I see," hissed my seatmate in whispered confidence.

I turned and risked a look at the features behind the venomous tone. Suddenly puzzled, and also curious as to her identity, I smiled tentatively at her, trying to match her face to chaotic ancient memories. But the database came up empty.

The applause ebbed.

"Please enjoy your luncheon," Peter said cajolingly from the podium. "We'll continue with pleasant reminiscences after dessert."

With that, an efficient flotilla of the club's catering staff descended on the assembled masses like a well-oiled convoy. For the next while, the room was filled with the muffled bustle of serving, dining, and clattering flatware, and humming conversations while gentle (if overly loud) music filtered through the sound system.

"Chopin, I think," volunteered my seatmate, her brows knitting in concentration. The four couples at our table, engaging each other in singular conversation, made it clear that they didn't know her either. As if realizing my thoughts, she held out her hand then and simply said, "I'm Florence, by the way."

There was nothing for it but to return the gesture, as I pulled the only name that came immediately to mind and nonsensically offered it in return:

"Joanna," I said, before adding "Just call me JoJo" as a filler. Well, Joanna wasn't a complete lie. It *was* my middle name, but where in the world had I pulled JoJo from?!

Her handshake was quick but firm. "You can call me Flo."

Was that said slyly? Or shyly? For an instant, I felt out of my element with no control of the situation.

For the next few moments, we occupied ourselves with mindless conversation about the weather, current fashions, and such—safe conventional topics that strangers gravitate towards when thrown into circumstances of close proximity.

"So, how long have you known Stuart and Adelaide?" Flo asked unexpectedly, while simultaneously digging into a sumptuous Greek salad.

This question out of left field caught me off guard. *Oh, God...* This was all my scrambled thoughts could muster. For the barest sliver of a second, my mind's eye recalled Adelaide's cruel dismissal of me from her inner circle all those years ago. Her determination had been that, since I would be of no use to her in climbing the social-ladder, I'd needed to simply vanish. The sheer public humiliation of this dismissal had eaten away at me for longer than I cared to remember.

Momentarily, my muddy thoughts cleared, and I rallied. "Oh, we go way back," I offered, breezily. "When our eldest were still toddlers." With that, wishing to turn any further questioning away from myself, I was emboldened to ask, "And you?"

"A bit further back than that, actually."

Ambiguous. Was it my imagination or had I sensed, or heard, a certain abstruse malevolence? I studied her expression, but her newly returned smile appeared authentic.

The overtures of Chopin, or whoever, still floated about the room more loudly than the atmosphere warranted, though it had become apparent that no one deemed it necessary to lower it a notch or two. Seeing an opportunity to use this to my advantage, I said, "Excuse me, but this music is playing havoc with my hearing aid." The lie in this statement seemed to echo loudly in my ears, but I pressed on, standing up and exiting swiftly to the ladies' room on the feeble pretext of rectifying the issue.

In truth, I did need a hearing aid, but I was still fighting my doctor's urging to obtain one, not wanting to get older any faster than necessary. Hearing aids were for really old people, I rationalized. Besides, as I'd confided to the shocked physician, "I've discovered that most people don't have much to say that I really want to hear!"

Thankfully, the powder room was unoccupied. Trying to figure out what to do next, I walked absently to the sink and automatically started washing my hands. Unconsciously raising my head, I caught a glimpse of myself in the mirror. My hands flew up instinctively to eradicate the bitter hatred the looking glass had captured, splashing drops of water everywhere. My head reeling, I blinked rapidly, trying to erase the image from my mind. Only as I heard the door open behind me did I break my stance. I couldn't get out of the room fast enough.

My plan was not to return to the table, but I soon found that I had to. In my hasty retreat, I had forgotten my clutch. Except for the fact that my key ring was inside it, I probably would have bolted from the building without it.

As I sat back down, Flo glanced at me. "Stuey doesn't look at all well. Seems positively stunted. What the hell has that bitch done to him?!"

This time, no attempt was made to buffer her malice. I didn't know what to say, so instead turned around and found my eyes drawn almost mechanically to Stuart at the front of the room. All these years, and he had never crossed my mind once. Only Adelaide. I found myself silently agreeing with Flo's assessment of him. This Stuart bore no resemblance to the brash, flashy guy I'd preserved in my memory banks.

All of a sudden, it struck me. *Stuey?* With that single utterance, I realized who Flo had to be. There had only ever been one person who called him that. Adelaide had even taken her to task on the issue, with acid in her tone. "Flo" was Stuart's sister, Violet!

Damn!

We'd even met once. She'd lived down East or somewhere and come home for a short visit. I swallowed hard, realizing that if I remembered her, it would only be a moment or two before she was able to place *me* as well. I was Isabella...the disgraced. I suddenly couldn't breathe!

"Excuse me another moment," I murmured in a low tone, and before Flo/Violet could speak, I picked up my clutch, rose, and walked briskly out of the main ballroom into the nearly deserted hallway outside.

"Oh, God," I muttered aloud, then swiftly glanced around. No one was within earshot. *What the hell am I doing here?* I asked myself in a sudden moment of lucidity. *Who the hell are you?* The memory of my hateful reflection in the bathroom mirror plucked powerfully at my consciousness.

I had been carrying my hatred of Adelaide around with me for so long now that I didn't even recognize it anymore. I had pinned an entirely different label onto what I was doing in order to right my perception of a deep-rooted wrong.

Justice.

Delving hard inside myself, I forced an ugly truth to the surface. Justice had nothing whatsoever to do with my actions. All it really came down to was ugly, petty revenge. Simple.

Except vengeance is never simple.

A tremendous urge to run filled me then. Taking a couple of deep breaths, I forced myself into calmness, and with every ounce of will-power I possessed, I stepped casually back into the ballroom. There was something I had to do. I just needed an opportune moment, which soon came in the form of a sudden (and blessedly short) speech from Peter, lavishing generous praise on the staff for a wonderful meal. A lusty round of applause followed. That was my cue.

Shuffling over to the gift table and the girl seated beside it, I fumbled about in the best interpretation of a doddering senior that I could muster.

"Oh, my goodness, my dear! I just remembered that I forgot to include the gift card in sweet Addy's envelope! Can you imagine that?!" I blubbered.

The teen's slightly bemused expression was conclusive enough to confirm that she could indeed believe my confusion and had no trouble imagining the mistake. Managing a small smile, she turned to look at the mountain of gifts as if in search of the right one.

"Um…which one—?"

"No need to trouble yourself, dear," I said, swiftly interrupting. "I see it just on the end there." Before she could utter another syllable, I snatched it from the table and hurriedly stuffed it inside my clutch.

"I shall have to go home and see if I can find that card. Oh, dear me! I wonder where I put my keys," I rattled on in visible agitation, even while turning away from the table.

Purposely doddering hesitantly out of the room, I half-expected someone to grab me at any instant and accuse me of theft. Nothing happened. Once outside, it was all I could do to refrain from sprinting across the parking lot. I say sprint, but of course, it probably would have been more of a "lope." At best.

With my clutch held tightly in my grip, I located my car, and without a backward glance, I climbed in and drove out of the lot. My heart was racing as I drove about a dozen blocks in the wrong direction, believing that some security guard—or heaven forbid, the police—would be right behind me!

Seeing no pursuit, I then turned around and drove home, taking the most circuitous route I could think of, my active imagination remaining vividly intact. Finally, I pulled into my driveway and parked, taking a few moments to quell my quivering as shame and disgust rattled over me. How had I allowed Adelaide to run amuck inside my skull for so long?

Once inside the house, I barely acknowledged a jubilant Dixie as I rushed into my makeshift office. Ripping the ribbon from the gift, I forced both the wrapping paper and envelope through the paper shredder's narrow opening, followed by the photographs (with accompanying negatives) chronicling Adelaide's youthful Wednesday afternoon romps at the Sweet Escapes Motel. *"I just wanted a few memories,"* she'd giggled while sharing them with me. *"I'll get them back from you in a little while."*

She'd never mentioned them again.

The shredding took less than a minute. Then I fell back into my office chair, my senses completely drained.

Dixie's animated hopping broke my trance.

"Hey, girl," I murmured distractedly, absently caressing her head and neck. I stood up then, shucking off my dress and donning comfy sweats. Then leaning over, I cupped her eager face in my hands and asked softly, "How about a couple of treats, hey?"

Her prancing turned to dancing at this suggestion.

I smiled as something akin to joy welled up inside me. I couldn't explain it. I felt…different somehow. *Free.* That was it. A schmalzy, happy, *movie* kind of feeling.

I couldn't remember when I had last felt this way, but apparently all it had taken to experience it again was a mirrored reflection, the passing of forty years, and a paper shredder.

Who knew?!

Some Such Something

*H**usbands are a piece of work*, I decided, firmly. *A damn sight too big a piece*, I added silently as a mix of sadness and anger washed over me.

I tried to focus on my actual work. My job, that is, which right now was attempting to wrangle the legal financial jargon intrinsic to the merger of two medium-sized plastics firms. Flashing continuously into the middle of these thoughts was the muddle of my impending divorce.

I was exhausted. Or maybe depressed.

What I'm trying to say is that I was still reeling from Dwayne's announcement some months back of his dalliance (yes, he used that word) with a now heavily pregnant little dolly—*my* word—and that he wanted to "do the right thing and marry her." I hadn't even realized that our own marriage was in trouble! And besides that, she was half his age! *Half* your *age,* my analytical brain blustered at me.

Removing my glasses, I pinched the bridge of my nose in an effort to forestall a threatening headache. My private desk line rang, and I recognized the number as belonging to Rosamund. My brow puckered. *Odd that she should call me at work*, I thought as I picked up.

"Hello," I answered, in the same instant wondering inanely where that greeting had originated. At the very least, it seems a bit odd putting "Hell" and "O" together to announce yourself. *Of course, I could Google it. If I remember to, that is. Fat chance of that.*

"Hi, Tessa. Sorry to bother you at work, but I need to ask you something," she said a bit breathlessly.

"Sure, Rosamund," I answered, somewhat puzzled, thinking only that she wanted to change the date of our next girls' night out. It was difficult coordinating four working women a month in advance.

"It's a *huge* favour," she stressed.

"Okay, sure. What exactly?"

She paused, and then in a detached sort of voice, said, "Can you come with me to a funeral?"

"A *funeral?* Oh my God! Who?" All other thoughts evaporated. "Who?" I repeated, hardly able to breathe.

"It's actually out west. In Edmonton, as a matter of fact. Can you come with me?"

"Edmonton? When?"

"We'd have to leave tomorrow. The funeral's on Saturday. I know it's the long weekend and all, and you probably have plans…but I wouldn't ask if it wasn't important."

My thoughts scattered like dust. I forced them quickly back into a regimented order I could make sense of. Dwayne and I normally went to the cabin for the July long weekend. I remembered that "normally" no longer existed, though, and forced my thoughts down a different path. It was just as well that tomorrow is Friday. You can't get any work out of anyone on a Friday. Combine that with a summer long weekend, and it's nigh impossible. Half the office staff had already booked off early.

"Sure. Okay. I can do it," I said, mentally sorting through logistics.

A huge rush of breath on the line greeted me as she began gushing with gratitude. "That's great, Tessa! You have no *idea* what this means to me. Thank you! Of course, I'll pay for your flight and accommodations—"

"You'll do no such thing," I said quickly, cutting her off. "Dwayne's going to be paying heftily for his little folly" —*dalliance*— "and this weekend is his treat."

She laughed a bit, then sobered and said, "No, that doesn't sound fair somehow and—"

"Fair isn't coming into anything right now. It's totally fine. Besides, it might be easier for me to book the flight. It's the long weekend, after all. Not sure what kind of luck I'll even have, but I fly all the time, so I should be able to swing something. We'll chat as soon as I can get things organized, okay?"

"Are you sure? I'm not trying to pass the legwork on to you."

"I'm sure," I answered firmly. Already, my headache was receding. Apparently, I'd just needed something else to focus on besides the sorry state of my own soon-to-be-former life.

I was about to hang up when I realized that Rosamund hadn't answered my question.

"Wait….Whose funeral is it?"

After a slight pause, she said, "One of my ex-brothers."

And with that, she hung up the phone.

✳ ✳ ✳

I HAD A THOUSAND QUESTIONS, but as it turned out, we never got a chance to chat at all.

To anyone who has never flown the width of Canada, let me explain something: The cost for a well-planned early booked flight can sometimes approach the same price as an online junker car, and with that option, you can at least use the car again. Obtaining a last-minute flight on the Friday of the July long weekend, though, is akin to winning the lottery. Doesn't happen. Or if it does, it's to people you've only been told about in stories you suspect are probably not true anyway.

But some seating designated "compassionate" can still be wrangled if you know how. And who better than a lawyer to wrangle something like that, right? Actually, to be honest, I can't even arrange a cab without the help of my secretary. I do, however, know a tremendous travel agent, who'd managed to get me on some other finicky flights in the past.

* * *

"JAMES, YOU'RE A JEWEL!" I enthused, calling him after I received his email confirmation with the flight details. "I'd name my first-born after you if it wasn't already years too late for that. I owe you. Big time. Thanks!"

He chuckled on the other end of the line. "Just remember me the next time you're tempted to book your vacation online. Online never gives personal service."

"You're my guy," I oozed. I couldn't wait to send the travel info along to Rosamund.

Needless to say, she was ecstatic, but there was no time to talk. For either of us. Packing took precedence. I slept little that night, a thousand questions tumbling and tumbling around in my mind.

* * *

AT FIVE A.M. ON FRIDAY, Rosamund and I met at Toronto airport's security check-in. One thing plain about last-minute bookings—even compassionate last-minute ones—is that we didn't get to sit together. I was plunked into the window seat beside a frantic young mother, an energetic toddler, and a colicky newborn. Rosamund's luck was little better. She was in the middle seat between two burly businessmen extending their bodily masses beyond their seats' capacities and into hers. Whereas I could always wear ear plugs, there was only so much that she could shrink.

* * *

A HOT JULY SUN ASSAILED us as we alighted from our cab outside the Varscona. The hotel lobby was headily scented with oranges and cinnamon. Taking deep breaths, we shared a small laugh. We'd made it! Our travel trials aside, we both agreed that a long lunch beckoned.

An hour later, we were sitting on the patio of a shady Whyte Avenue pub, enjoying glasses of wine and delicious salads. As usual, summer in Canada was showcasing all manner of individual choices of summer dress (and undress). Some chosen styles we spotted around us were interesting, in a *"Hmmm, what was she thinking?"* kind of way. Others were eye-popping, meriting barely concealed smiles and lively comments.

Knowing that the subject of the funeral itself would have to wait until my lunch companion was ready to discuss it, I allowed myself to relax and just look at my friend.

Rosamund wasn't what one would term beautiful in any traditional sense, but she still drew glances wherever she went, all of which she seemed entirely oblivious to. Perhaps that was part of the charm. Innocence can be magic. Today, though, there was a heightened sense of something else in her demeanour. Different from what I would have considered any part of her daily character. Was it fear? I could almost hear her heart pounding.

She took a small sip of wine, set down her glass, and looked around. "I was never allowed in this part of the city when I was young. My parents said it was filled with too many undesirables. Or some such thing. Something like that, anyway." She paused, taking a deep breath, and as she did so, the scent of her perfume wafted across the table.

"Tessa," she said then, before I could comment on the lovely fragrance, and an earnestness clouded her features, "I know you will think me the oddest duck, but I need to ask you one further favour."

"Of course."

"First of all, do you know why I asked *you* to come here with me and not Heather or Susan?"

"I assume," I answered lightly, "because of my quiet and unassuming nature and the fact that I rarely speak my mind or put the truth on display." I was glad when she smiled. "Or maybe," I continued, scrounging up a deliberate scowl, "so that I—a bona-fide easterner—will be able to attest first-hand to the fact that the western cowboy region of this country is not just frozen tundra full of uneducated and senseless thugs with whom we privileged easterners are much too high brow to associate. But as you know, I'm *much* too genteel to mention such things and always keep my negative opinions to myself."

We both giggled with laughter, loudly enough that a few diners at adjacent tables looked our way and smiled.

Rosamund sobered then. "I actually wanted a methodical witness to study everyone at the funeral, or at the very least, to study my family's reaction when they see that I've come to it."

I was a bit stunned. "I know you haven't had actual contact with your family for years, but they know you're coming, right? I mean, someone called and asked you to come because it's your brother that died. That's right, isn't it?"

Rosamund hesitated but was only able to muster a single soft-spoken word: "No."

18

"How did you know, then? Facebook or something?"

She sighed. "Basically, a friend of a friend of a former friend heard about it and told me."

"So, *no one* knows or is expecting you?" I said, putting it right out there. "Is that what you're saying?"

"Yes," she said in a small voice. "I guess that's it."

"Rosamund, you're like a sister to me. Basically, the sister I would have picked, if given a choice. But honestly? Sometimes I can't figure you out. What do you hope to gain by 'dropping in' like this? That they'll look at you and be so glad to see you that they welcome you back? That it'll be all sunshine and kisses and wishes that they'd seen you years ago? Is that what you think is going to happen?"

By her stricken expression and welling tears, I knew that I'd accidentally hit the nail right on the head.

Seeing her lip start to quiver, I sighed quietly and worked to soften my tone. "Rosamund, it won't happen that way. Deep down, you *must* know that. The best that could come out of this is them being surprised and grudgingly asking you to sit with them. Or perhaps even making false statements about how happy they are that you came and how glad they are to see you. Insincere stuff like if they'd known how to get in touch with you, they would have let you know. Blah, blah, blah. The usual nonsense people say that generally means nothing. But the *worst* that could happen would be you getting totally shunned, which would kill you. I know you well enough to know that."

With tears still threatening to spill, she said nothing.

After a long, quiet moment, I suddenly got a better idea and told her as much, though she just looked at me as if hoping for a miracle.

"I need to buy a suitcase," I said.

"A suitcase?" she repeated, frowning liberally at me as though I'd lost my mind.

"Well, yeah. This is Alberta, right? No provincial sales tax. I think shopping is on the agenda. Shopping and definitely a late-night pub crawl. Maybe even some cowboy music." I glanced around. "I can see a bar down the street that looks like just the place. A perfect neighbourhood for a couple of undesirables like us. And it's close enough to the hotel that we could actually *really* crawl home if we had to."

I needed her to see the futility of what she had hoped to accomplish, hoping that my meagre attempt at humour would change her outlook from fairy tale to reality. Or (at least) convince her to do *anything* besides actually attending this ex-brother's funeral.

She shook her head tiredly. "You're crazy. Tessa, we just flew all the way across the country! And for what? Shopping? You're nuts!"

"No nuttier than what you're planning," I continued, soberly. "I know the herculean efforts it took to separate yourself from your toxic family, and that they've always treated you as if you had some monstrous plague. Your only link to your brothers is biological at this point. Your parents had sex and produced a few by-products. That's all. A shared bloodline is a fine starting point for families, but it isn't the only one. You're a treasure, Rosamund, and they'll only try to wipe that out again, and maybe even succeed this time. It's not worth it. *They're* not worth it. Even if they'd actually tracked you down and *invited* you to the funeral, I wouldn't necessarily support you going. With today's technology, I'm sure they could have found you if they'd tried, but they didn't do that. Did they?"

She shook her head and bit her lip anxiously. Then she looked around. "Shopping…" Glancing at me, a wane smile struggled to exert itself then. "You know what that means for me too, don't you?"

I shrugged.

Her smile widened. "I really need to buy a suitcase!"

"Well," I said happily, jumping in and trying to keep the levity flowing, "like I said, there's no sales tax here! Alberta's the place to buy, alright! Besides, imagine the story we'll have to tell Heather and Susan next week at girls' night. If you think *I'm* nuts, just wait 'til the two of them gang up on us, telling us what fruitcakes both of us are!"

She groaned loudly then. "I feel like an idiot. I've dragged you out here and—"

"That's enough of that," I scolded her softly. "It's time to go shopping. I hear there are even a couple stores here and there. I think there's some big mall or something, right?" I teased.

"Oh, Tessa, I'm *so* glad you came. I would have made a total fool of myself, wouldn't I?"

"We all do that from time to time," I said. My thoughts crossed momentarily over to Dwayne and me, and sadness threatened. Blinking it away, I looked around and added laughingly, "So…I have one pressing question for you: How come I haven't seen any cowboys yet?"

Double Whammy

ABBY WAS BORED. BEYOND BORED. She sighed audibly, absolutely, genuinely relieved that the annual ten-kilometre fun run had been postponed due to the day's rainy forecast. She didn't want to participate any longer anyway. It had all become so tedious and repetitive, with the same people every year and all of them endlessly boring, boring, boring.

Time to focus her energies on another challenge.

She opened her mouth to voice these thoughts to Pete, but her husband was already embroiled in an argument on his cell:

"Damn it, Josh! You've got to keep on top of those guys! Okay, okay, we'll work it out! I'm just leaving!" With that, he gave Abby a quick kiss and was gone.

A horn honked. The school bus!

"Hurry up, you two!" Abby yelled.

Jamming on runners and stuffing his homework into a backpack, Jeremy rushed for the door, but Lena shoved him aside, pushing through ahead of him, throwing barbed comments at her younger brother all the while—comments that were silenced finally by the door slamming shut behind them.

"Have a great day, everyone!" Abby said loudly to the closed door.

Her cell rang. It was Bobby.

"Sorry, sis," he said hurriedly. "I have to cancel tonight. I'll make it up to you, okay?"

"Okay," was all she managed to get out before he hung up the phone, and then he too was gone.

Sheesh, she thought, her brow furrowing. *Does no one have a minute to talk today?*

Frowning, she plunked herself on a kitchen chair, wrapping her hands around a coffee mug. Bobby had cancelled on a few family events lately. *Julie again?* she thought, knowing that she should be happy that (maybe) he was finally getting a life. Since Sarah had left him, he'd more or less buried himself in his work. *But...Julie? Really?* She'd tried talking to Pete about it, but he had said more than once, "Bobby's a big boy. He can take care of himself. Besides, Abby, it's none of your business."

"He's my brother," she'd always retorted. "Of *course* it's my business!"

And then he would shake his head. "Stay out of it, Abby!"

Pushing Pete's advice aside, she impulsively scrolled her cell for Julie's number. Barely taking time to reflect on her action, she pressed her number.

"Hello?" said a child's voice on the line as barking dogs echoed in the background.

"Hello. Could I speak with your mom, please?" Abby asked, knowing it was now too late to hang up.

"Mommy, it's for you!" yelled the child, followed by a noticeable clattering.

"Hello?" Abby repeated after a moment as the canine crescendo in the background began to diminish somewhat.

Suddenly, Julie was on the line. "Hi, Abby. Sorry about that. I've been trying to teach Eloise how to properly handle a phone call."

"Hey, Julie, I've actually been meaning to call for a long while now. Thought we could maybe get together today and do lunch? I know it's short notice, but it would be great to see you," Abby added sweetly, hoping the string of lies sounded truthful on the other end.

After a brief hesitation, Julie replied, "Uh, thanks…Well, that *does* sound nice. Really. Thanks. I haven't done a lunch for a bit. Outside of occasional fast-food with the kids, anyway. It's my only day off this week, and I'm not sure I can get a sitter, but I can give it a try." She sounded nervous. "Okay if I call you back in a minute?"

JULIE'S MINUTE HAD ENDED UP being closer to twenty, but she had managed to arrange a sitter, and a few hours later, Abby and Julie arrived at the Polka Dot almost simultaneously, dashing into the café just as the predicted rain began to fall.

The restaurant had been recently renovated, and Abby loved it. The fifties ambiance had been retained, though its faded blue had been replaced with a cheery red. The most important thing about "the Dot" had always been its location though, with its enviable panoramic view of the town and valley below. Of course, today, with the rain, the view was not quite as idyllic as normal. A popular spot for lunch, the Dot was crowded and bustling. Abby deliberately waved to everyone she knew, wanting to impress Julie, though she wasn't sure why. Scurrying towards a recently vacated booth, Julie never even noticed.

Damn, she thought.

They each ordered a quiche and tossed salad. Abby added a bottle of the house red. Julie pooh-poohed the wine, but Abby insisted. "My treat."

Julie acquiesced reluctantly. "Okay. One glass."

Initial conversation was a trifle awkward, but a few sips of wine combined with the excellent quiche soon contributed to an easier flow of banter. Conversation centred mostly around kids and school at first but soon shifted gradually towards old times as they enjoyed an excellent lunch. According to the large wall clock, it was just after one o'clock when the lunch rush ended, with most of the tables emptying as tabs were paid and tables cleared away.

But Abby was ready to top up both of their glasses.

"Actually, don't, please," Julie protested. "I really have to go soon. One glass is generally my limit."

Abby shrugged, not ready to give up her hope that the alcohol might help steer the conversation where she was hoping to take it. "Heck, there's only a little left. What about just a *small* second glass?"

"No, really," Julie said firmly. "Next time, maybe."

Abby was horrified at this suggestion and silently vowed that there would *be* no second time, even as she returned a dazzling smile to Julie, or at least what she hoped was a dazzling smile. Even though she hated to admit it, she couldn't help but marvel that Julie had managed to keep her figure after four kids. *My God, who has four kids nowadays? I mean, really? Ever heard of birth control? Geez!* Remembering that Julie was raising this brood of children on her own after her divorce, Abby suddenly felt very smug about her own life.

"I really should go," Julie declared again, comparing the time on her watch with the accuracy of the wall clock.

"Oh, it's fine," Abby rebutted. "Just give the sitter a call and let her know you'll be a little late."

Julie paused a second before saying, "I actually couldn't *get* a sitter." Somewhat sheepishly, she added, "I was about to call you back to cancel when Bobby rang. He's keeping an eye on Eloise."

Abby was shocked. *Bobby babysitting?! What the hell is going on?!*

She couldn't hold back any longer. Everything she'd been thinking suddenly spilled out from behind the wall of expensively straightened teeth that could no longer maintain the false smile. "What the hell is going on with you and Bobby anyway?"

Julie gasped, even as Abby's hand flew to her mouth, her eyes widening as she realized what she'd just said. It wasn't supposed to come out like that! Bobby was going to kill her! Not to mention what Pete was going to say!

There was a small silence, then Julie responded stiffly: "I wondered what this invite was all about. Bobby said that you were going to ask me something like that, but I really didn't believe him! If I'd taken the time to think about it, I should have known that you would never invite me for lunch just because you wanted to see me. We weren't even friends at school, but still, I thought that maybe you wanted to chat because…well, because Bobby and I are friends."

"Friends? Is that what they call it these days?" *Oh my God, did I really just say that!* Abby was aghast, certain that she was going straight to hell! *What is happening?!* With a shaking hand, she took a gulp of wine, thinking it might somehow quell any further verbal outbreaks. Then she sank back in the booth, realizing that her brother was definitely going to kill her!

"Seriously, Abby? What's between Bobby and me is none of your business!"

For once, Abby found herself at a loss for words. She could barely even look at her lunch partner.

Julie sighed and shook her head. "Bobby said that if you were your 'usual nosy, bossy self' —his words, not mine—I should just tell you everything and get it over with."

Abby's eyes had widened at the insulting quote from Bobby, but her natural curiosity wouldn't allow her to remain silent. "Tell me what?"

Julie shook her head again. "Boy, you haven't changed at all. Still sticking your nose in! Might as well tell you or else you'll probably go straight to Bobby and bug him about it." She took a deep breath, and then said simply, "Your brother's repaying a debt that he thinks he owes me."

"What debt?" Abby said derisively. "What could he *possibly* owe you?"

Julie huffed at this, rolling her eyes. "I said that he *thinks* he owes me a debt. Don't you ever just listen?!" Before Abby could respond, Julie shook her head brusquely. "Never mind!" She started to slide to the edge of the booth. "I have to go!"

With that, she made as if to stand up, but Abby reached across the table, touching her hand and giving her an imploring look. "Please, don't go. I'm sorry. Please." She really did feel sorrier than she could even say, knowing that she'd handled this poorly.

Julie looked at her for a moment, and then sat back. "I should just walk out and say to hell with you."

"I wouldn't blame you if you did," she replied somberly.

Julie gave her another look, and then seemed to come to a decision. Crossing her arms across her chest, she started to explain: "It was a Saturday night, the summer after grade nine. I was out with a bunch of kids. Most of them were older than me, and several were the same sort of slick and useless guys I'm typically attracted to. We were out by Big Creek, drinking and racing across the dunes."

She paused a moment, staring out through the rain-streaked windows as if reliving the day in question. When she started speaking again, her voice had grown quiet. "After awhile, everyone got bored and most of them left. In the end, there was just me and Joe Stedsbury...and Bobby."

"Bobby!"

Julie nodded. "He must have gotten a ride with someone because Joe's beater car was the only vehicle there at this point. I hadn't even noticed Bobby at all before that. Though I didn't know it at the time, not long ago, he told me that the reason he stayed was because he didn't want to leave me alone with Joe, who had kind of a wild reputation with the girls."

"I remember," Abby said grimly, giving Julie a knowing look.

"Really? You and Joe? Wow!" Julie stifled a giggle then and added playfully, "He obviously had some good taste then, right?"

"Hmmm." A flush of colour rose in Abby's cheeks as she consciously pushed aside encroaching memories.

"Anyway," Julie continued after a moment, her tone sobering, "Joe suddenly pulled out this rifle he had with him in his car. I think it was a BB gun or maybe a .22. Nothing extreme."

Abby shivered as a flicker of fear coursed through her, but she remained silent as Julie continued.

"Looking at Bobby and me, he suggested that we shoot at a few cars on the highway. It was basically a dare sort of thing, so of course, I said that I was game. I'd been drinking, after all, and more or less drunk, but I was also trying to impress him. Bobby said no right off. He said that it was stupid and dangerous and asked Joe what the hell he was thinking. Joe got a bit mad, and eventually, Bobby agreed to go along with him, but I think that was mostly because…well, Joe was holding a gun; wasn't he? Anyway, the three of us got in Joe's car and drove to the nearest range road, which Joe declared was as good as a highway.

"Not far from the old dump, I think, he pulled off into the ditch, and we all got out. When the first car passed, Joe shot at it. He missed, and the car just kept going. He handed the rifle to me, but guns scared the pants right off me. Still do. I was sobering up a bit by this time though, because when the next vehicle came, I fired wildly in the complete opposite direction.

"At that point, Joe started going on and on at me about how stupid I was, and then made a grab for the gun. Bobby beat him to it, and after a bit of a tussle between them, Bobby ended up with it."

Time had stopped for Abby as this story unfolded. Everything stopped. This was about her perfect older brother!

As though she could read Abby's thoughts, Julie gave her a look. "That's right, Bobby. Mr. Brainy with the top grades, in all the clubs at school, and the poster boy for teacher's pet. He had the rifle in his hands, and I think he was just trying to figure out how to get out of there when another vehicle came around the bend. Somehow, the driver saw us and braked hard in the gravel, crunching to a stop. It was old man Silas, and he got out of his pickup fast, swearing something fierce!

"Joe jumped back into his own car, but Bobby was kind of in shock and just stood for a second or two, still holding that damn rifle! Then suddenly, he was yelling at me to get in the car, and I was actually arguing with him! I just refused, telling him wildly that *no one* was going to tell *me* what to do! For some unfathomable reason, I even snatched the rifle from him and started waving it around, ordering Bobby to get in the car.

"Joe was bellowing at us both, and with all the chaos and Albert Silas nearly on top of us, Bobby finally hopped into the front passenger seat and hollered for me to get in the back. I was just about to grab the rear door handle when Joe blasted that car out of the ditch like hell itself was behind him."

Julie took a long slow breath, and then continued, still absently staring out the window at the rainy day. "He left me standing there like an idiot with that bloody gun!" She shook her head slowly. "I couldn't quite believe he'd done it and was still processing when Silas grabbed the gun and twisted my arm up behind me...even as a couple of the town cops pulled up. I heard later that the driver of the first car had gone straight to the cop shop and lodged a complaint.

"Anyway, I was hauled in and told that I could be charged with…I don't even know what anymore. They said it would go easier on me if I told them who else had been there. I insisted that there had been no one. Since Mr. Silas was unable to identify the guys or their vehicle, and I opted to stick to my story, I ended up with a million hours of community service…or that's what it felt like anyway. I worked at that crap rec centre every Friday and Saturday night for the next six months, cleaning bathrooms and sweeping up. And boy, let me tell you, some people are pigs!"

She sighed, uncrossing her arms and leaning her elbows on the table, though her eyes never left the window. "When my folks picked me up from the police station…well, they laughed it off to the cops, as though it was nothing, what I'd done. After they got me home though, I found out what 'nothing' really meant. Believe me, I got the belt but good." She stopped and tried to laugh even as she blinked back tears.

Abby was so quiet that if it weren't for the low hum of the fifties tune playing on the jukebox, you could have heard a pin drop. Finally, she said, "You never said anything about anyone else being there?"

"No," Julie said, giving her a look. "Why would I? Keeping quiet had made me Joe's hero. Well, for about two weeks, anyway, until he hooked up with Maggie…or whoever." She frowned at this. "Funny," she mused, "I don't even remember who it was anymore!"

Abby didn't know if she wanted to hear any more but figured it was too late to back out now. "And Bobby?"

"Bobby came to see me the next day. I was more embarrassed about the state of the house than anything. My parents were drinking, as usual, but I was thankful they were down at the bar and not at home. He wanted to somehow make it up to me. Said he'd go to the police and say it was him, but I convinced him to leave it, that I was fine the way it was, and that this was what I wanted. He really didn't want to, but eventually he agreed. About a month or so later, he stopped by again. I remember thinking, *Crap,* because this time, my folks were home. Anyway, he said that he had something to tell me that I deserved to hear first, before he told anyone else: He'd just won a big scholarship, one he hadn't expected. They'd apparently done a background check on him to make sure that he deserved it and had found nothing bad. And that was because of me. He said that he owed me, and I told him that he didn't, especially since he'd been willing to come forward and admit to having been there that night. We were totally square."

"That was a $50,000 scholarship," Abby said quietly, remembering Bobby saying at the time that he hadn't thought he'd even had a chance. "He was the first kid from a small town to ever win it." She suddenly realized that without Julie staying quiet, he would have lost that chance for certain.

Julie nodded, and then shrugged. "Yeah, well…The following year when I was with Jack Reardon—you don't know him—I got pregnant. So, we got married and moved down east, but he left me and the kids a few years later. Said he couldn't handle the pressure of marriage and everything." She paused. "The rest is history. I moved back home with the kids when money got tight. Didn't want to, but I had to go somewhere. Bobby came to see me not long after, saying that he wanted to repay the debt. I asked him, 'What debt?' The whole gun thing seemed a lifetime ago by that point, but he reminded me how much it had meant to him. I told him again that he didn't owe me anything. That it was all okay. But you know Bobby. He can get pretty determined."

Too true, agreed Abby, silently.

"Anyway, he kind of got out of me the fact that I wasn't too thrilled to be back with my folks, and he mentioned an idea that he had." Her voice became more animated as a smile returned to her features, widening as she continued. "It was a real sweet deal that will see me getting in on buying one of the houses he's building in the new sub-division on the hill. An honest-to-goodness brand-new house, Abby! I couldn't turn that down, could I?"

She looked at Abby now, sighing and shrugging again, her voice sobering once more. "I'd like to say that I've agreed just for the kids, but that wouldn't be totally true. It's for me too. I'm saving what I can for the down payment, once it's finished, and will be paying the mortgage *myself*. On my really down days, juggling two jobs and having no extra money, I remember that something good had finally come of all that stuff that happened way back when. Makes everything seem a bit easier." She stopped speaking then as tears were threatening to spill from her eyes. She blinked them away and stared out the window again.

Abby didn't know what to say, so she just sat there for a moment before rousing herself enough to send a quick text. When she was done, she placed her phone down on the table and looked at Julie.

"I ordered a cab. I'm thinking neither of us should be driving right now. Me, for sure. A bit too much wine," she confessed, laughing a little before adding softly, "Thank you, Julie, for what you did for Bobby. He's kind of my hero. I always thought of him as basically being perfect."

"No one's perfect," Julie said, "though Bobby is one of the good ones." She looked back across the table with a thoughtful expression. "So, Abby, I'm guessing that's about the closest to an apology I'm going to get from you for conning me into this lunch. Am I right?"

"No, it isn't." Abby leaned across the table and stared earnestly into Julie's face, "I *am* sorry for tricking you, but I'm *so* glad you told me all of that. Otherwise, I'd still be trying to figure out what the *bleep* is going on and driving myself to distraction." She paused and added with full sincerity, "I don't know of a single other person who would have done what you did. I don't even know if I would have. I like to think I would, but I don't know. Maybe we can start again, and this time really be friends. Good friends."

Abby glanced out the window then, noticing that the cab had already arrived. *It must have been close.* "We can talk more about that later," she said. "Our ride's here."

Julie smiled, her eyes narrowing. "Okay, but just to clarify something: That part about us being friends…You sure that isn't just the cheap house wine talking?"

"No," Abby answered insistently. "Not at all!"

"So…" Julie began slowly, "if I were to tell you that Bobby and I are together, more than just friends, I mean…you'd be okay with that, right? We were going to wait awhile before saying anything, but he did say I could tell you everything. The past and the present. You're okay with it then? Him and me?" She stopped, studying Abby's expression.

Abby's eyes widened. "Uh…of-of course," she stammered. "But I know you're just joking." Her voice sounded somewhat strangled. "You're not actually with him."

"Why not, Abby?" she asked, watching her carefully. "You and I are friends now, right? You'd be happy for Bobby and me, wouldn't you?"

Abby's breathing was becoming laboured. "You're just joking, right? Anyway, Bobby wouldn't—" She snapped her mouth shut, stopping herself before she revealed too much.

"Wouldn't what? Hmmm? Wouldn't be with someone like me?" Julie's eyes hardened as she continued, her tone ice. "With some lowlife from a trash family with a bunch of kids and a loser ex-husband? Is that what you're saying?"

Abby said nothing, her mouth suddenly dry. She swallowed hard, her eyes darting everywhere. When the cab's horn sounded from outside, Abby quickly grabbed her phone. "I've got to go," she said flatly. "It's probably best that you get your own cab."

"No problem," Julie said easily, giving her a rigid look. "If I need a ride, I'll just call Bobby and get him to pick me up."

"Leave Bobby alone, Julie!" Abby hissed. "He's a good guy. He didn't deserve that ungrateful Sarah, and he certainly deserves better than—" She stopped herself again, knowing that she'd already pushed far beyond any remaining fragments of decency. And certainly, well past the point of redemption.

"So, having saved your brother's neck a long time ago, and telling you about it, I'm now worthy of being your good friend…but I'm still not good enough for your brother." Julie leaned closer. "Have I got that right? After all, no one else knows what I did for him, and heaven forbid you were forced to explain to anyone that he owes the wonderful, successful life he has now to a nobody like me."

Glaring at her hatefully, Abby stood up and left the Dot, sprinting through the downpour and into the cab.

Pensively watching as the cab pulled away, Julie murmured, "Maybe Joe didn't have such great taste after all."

Then There's Nora

EVERY NOW AND THEN, I like to get together with three of my friends for a boys' night out, full of hard-hitting poker, greasy take-out, and pricy scotch. And almost every time, a couple of drinks in, a sort of one-upmanship manages to creep in, with each of us bragging about who among us is the better "wheeler-dealer." Perhaps not unsurprisingly, such evenings habitually end on a sour note.

Amidst all the hyped-up blustering and posturing, there is one thing that we all basically agree on though: Human nature, especially when it comes to money. It's as predictable as the sunrise.

"People are people." That was Artie McColl, his voice slurring as he set his glass down on the table. "You know what I'm talking about, right? If some guy sees twenty bucks on the floor, do you think he's going to holler, 'Hey, has anyone lost any money?' No way! He'll take a quick look around, and if no one's watching, he'll snatch it up fast and stuff it in his jeans!"

"Or Armani suit!" laughed Don Wheelding.

I smiled and nodded. *Absolutely!*

"Maybe," said Jim Overbody. "Maybe not. There might be some who wouldn't." Good old Jim. But then again, he also reckons that every hand he holds is a big win. Hasn't figured out that a poker win needs a poker face!

"Okay, Jimmy boy," prodded Don good-naturedly. "You know someone like that? Your spinster aunt maybe? Probably wasn't wearing her trifocals, is all!"

There was general amusement as we tossed our cards back for another shuffle.

"Care to make a serious wager on that?" offered Jim, casting a casual glance around the table.

The laughter stopped cold. We shared looks. *Hell, yeah!*

"Alright!" Artie began, rubbing his hands together gleefully. "The night's finally getting interesting! Well guys, if we're going to do this, let's make it worthwhile. What are we looking at here?"

Ideas churned as an hour spun by, at the end of which, Artie scratched a rudimentary outline on the back of a Louie's Fast Eats napkin.

"Okay, here's what we got," he said, summarizing the deal. "We each donate five thousand. Cash. Each five goes in a separate marked envelope. Every envelope is left somewhere to be found by a predesignated, randomly selected finder. The finder has four days to turn it in. Funds intact, of course. Those not returned are considered a poker loss. Any that are turned in will, in turn, be returned to the original donator. Donators whose envelopes are not returned pay an additional five grand to any donators whose envelopes are turned in. As per usual, to make sure no one's screwing anyone, we hire an impartial management firm to handle the details." He looked around. "Agreed?"

"What if all the finders turn their envelopes in?" Jim asked.

"Jimmy," I began patiently, wondering absently—and not for the first time—how he'd ever managed to turn his two-bit trucking company into a national behemoth, "we've all been around long enough to recognize that the chance of that is pretty damn slim. Actually, if I really think about it, they're basically nil. *But… if* that happens, everyone will just get their own money back. No winner. Yeah?"

Heads bobbed.

Suddenly, a more calculating idea took root in my thoughts. "Hey, what about adding another wrinkle to the pot, with any donators whose envelopes *aren't* turned in contributing an additional five to charity? That's a tax write-off, guys, no matter how you cut it. Helps defray the five grand lost. What do you think?"

"Typical Reg Hawthorne move," joked Artie, leaning back. "Always figuring in the extra-money angle."

I shrugged. "Why not?" *Who doesn't, right?*

In the end, everyone agreed, and the plan was set into motion.

* * *

WHEN IT WAS TIME TO learn the results, we met at Don's penthouse. Lots of leather, glass, and chrome. I conceded that its river view was stunning, but get me a little closer to grass and earth any day.

Joining our quartet was a striking redhead in turquoise-rimmed glasses and bespoke suit. "Good evening, gentlemen" she began with a dazzling smile. "I'm Sara Stanton, your representative from 'Anything Goes.'" With that, she immediately launched into an abbreviated version of her firm's doctrine, which was clearly catering to the whims of the wealthy, though she was astute enough to phrase it all in a rather more genteel manner.

All business, I thought. I liked that, though my jaw clenched when I recalled the outrageous fee that we'd been charged to have our little wager played out.

Sara dropped four individually numbered slips of paper from one to four into a small black box, and then after a few shakes of the lidded container, she passed it around. I drew number four.

Flipping open a laptop, she stated breezily, "I just want to add that this has personally been an extremely fascinating project." Her comment drew only tight looks and silence. Money was serious business.

Looking slightly flustered at our lack of response, her gaze dropped to the screen. The next couple of minutes was a recitation of her firm's stringent privacy and security protocols. Basically, 'blah, blah, blah.' You know, the usual stuff. Nothing I hadn't heard a hundred times before. Finally, she finished up: "Everything has been done to ensure complete confidentiality and strict anonymity of the four finders. Any questions?"

We shared looks and a couple of shrugs, but that was all.

"Alright, let's get started," Sara continued. "Who has number one?"

Don raised a hand, waving his bit of paper. "Number one," she repeated, "is male, fifty-three, and a self-employed home renovator. He spied the envelope, took a quick look around, picked it up, and went home."

So far, I thought, *human nature is right on the money.* I laughed inwardly at my unintended pun.

"The next day, he drove through his bank's drive-through wicket," she continued matter-of-factly. "From there, he headed across town to a sports and recreation outlet. The following day, his social-media account lauded a photo of his sleek new speedboat. No envelope was turned in within the agreed-upon four days," she concluded and paused.

"Damn," cursed Don softly, slumping dejectedly in his seat.

Sara glanced around, and then said, "Two?"

Jim nodded.

"Forty-one-year-old female airport worker. The envelope was retrieved, at which time she immediately hurried out of the building and drove home. She emerged a short while later with a couple of suitcases, loaded them in her car, and headed south on the freeway. To date, she hasn't been back, and no envelope was turned in."

"You've got a runner there, Jimmy!" Artie roared with a huge laugh.

Jim leapt to his feet, visibly agitated. Running his hands furiously over his head, he bellowed, "I should have known better than to get involved in this scam with you guys! It's all rigged, right? Right?" Anger laced his every word.

"What?" shouted Don. "You think we're conning you somehow? I just lost five thousand too, you little shi—"

"Gentlemen!" Sara said, her voice raised somewhat. "I can assure you everything has been done totally above board. All events have been taped and recorded to ensure full transparency of the entire process."

"Come on, guys," Artie interjected soothingly. "Let's just get this finished, okay? I've got number three," he added flatly.

Jim dropped heavily onto the sofa, staring morosely out the window.

"Number three," Sara stated, "is male, forty-eight, and a human-resources manager. The envelope was picked up, and then he went straight home. Nothing was turned in—"

"Maybe he's still thinking things over," Artie broke in excitedly, looking around for a buy-in to the idea.

"Nope!" Jim was emphatic. "Four days max, old buddy!"

"Actually, number three is currently on a Mexican vacation," explained Sara. "He did not turn in the envelope within the required time frame."

"Come on, guys," I said, in an effort to ease the friction. "Human nature, remember? This was all to prove a point, and now we're proving it. Why get bent out of shape over a few bucks? We've each lost more than ten times that on any number of deals over the years." I looked back at Sara and nodded. "Go on."

With a small, appreciative smile, she continued. "Number four was slated to be a female, sixty-nine-year-old retired accountant and part-time dog walker." She paused then as if contemplating her next words.

"And…?" That was Don, his tone frosty.

"The envelope was dropped right beside the driver's door of her vehicle just as she exited the mall, but we had a slight hiccup—"

"Hiccup?!" Artie blustered, his face contorting. "What hiccup?"

Avoiding any direct eye contact, she hurriedly resumed. "Well, she stopped outside the mall doors for a smoke. In the meantime, a minivan pulled up and parked beside her SUV. The driver exited, spied the envelope, picked it up, and re-entered her own vehicle. At that point, our operative couldn't see exactly what was happening, but it appeared as if she had opened the package. A minute later, she drove away."

A verbal tirade of foul language erupted from all four of us.

"Please, let me finish!" Sara said loudly, trying to be heard over the din. "I can explain."

"You damn well better," someone spit out.

Though clearly rattled, Sara managed to regain a small measure of her previous poise. "The whole incident happened so fast that our guy wasn't sure exactly what to do, but as soon as she pulled out, he followed her. Ten minutes later, she turned into a police station, parked, and went inside. To put it simply, the envelope was handed in at the front counter there." She stopped speaking then, her gaze settling on four stunned faces.

I was the first to voice what we were all thinking: "What about the money? Was it all there?"

"One corner of the envelope had been ripped open," she replied. "Just enough to see what was inside. That's all. Nothing was removed."

Another shocked silence.

Sara took advantage of the moment to get back to business. "Well, gentlemen, it's probably best to conclude this transaction. Numbers one, two, and three…" She paused briefly to consult her notes. "That's Misters Wheelding, Overbody, and McColl, each owe five thousand to the original pot, which is subsequently paid to Mr. Hawthorne. Added to this is a further five thousand from each to be donated to the agreed-upon charity."

"Son of a…Ole Reggie wins again," mumbled Artie dourly, shaking his head. "Oh well. Congrats, Reg."

"Yeah, same," muttered Don.

Jim managed a nod.

Sara held an envelope out to me. "Here's the returned five thousand, Mr. Hawthorne. My congratulations also, sir."

Sensing the room's tension, I changed tactics, holding the envelope back out to her. "Actually, I think that should be put with the other fifteen for charity. They can even have my winnings, and I'll add another five. Let's face it: They need the money more than we do."

The proverbial pin was heard dropping.

Had I lost my senses? Hardly. It was more an immediate realization that the wager's validity could be challenged. After all, it was someone other than the predesignated finder who had retrieved the envelope. As such, I had quickly concluded that the only defense was a solid offence. Since *everything* was now going to charity, none of them would begrudge it. My additional five grand was just icing on the cake to ensure it happened.

I'd won the bet. Period. End of story.

But really…it wasn't.

✳ ✳ ✳

A FEW WEEKS LATER, MY assistant buzzed my office, advising me that my anticipated visitor had arrived: Nora Corsiato. She was thirty-three years old, married with kids, and a part-time cashier at a supermarket chain.

She was also number four.

Anonymity, confidentiality, and human nature. A tantalizing combination. Sultry Sara had provided me with exactly the information I'd wanted despite her well-rehearsed security-protocol speech. All it had taken was money.

Nora entered.

I didn't know until that moment what I'd expected, but facing me was a pleasant smile in a faintly appealing face. Her firm handshake was also a surprise. Other than that, though, she was so…average. If I had subconsciously harboured any preconceived notions of her appearance, this had not been it.

I waved her into the visitor chair opposite me on the far side of my desk.

"Mr. Hawthorne," she began, a bit nervously, "thank you again for the glowing letter and five-hundred-dollar reward. I understand that you've already received my thank-you card, so I confess to being a bit confused as to why you wanted to meet with me."

"I just wanted to add my personal thanks," I said, smiling my most charming smile. "Not everyone would have done what you did."

"Oh, I don't know about that," she demurred, blushing.

Could she really be this naïve?

I didn't respond right away. Unsure of what else was expected of her, she said, "Well…if that's all, I really must be going."

As she rose to leave, I decided to be entirely candid with her. "I do have a question, if I may."

She nodded and sank back down.

"Why did you really turn that money in? Hell, nobody does that. Nobody. Trust me on that."

She looked surprised. Even taken aback. Her quizzical look fell away, only to be replaced with a look that I struggled to identify. *Is that surprise? Disappointment?* Whatever it was, it disappeared before I had a chance to reflect on it any further, though I had the sudden uncomfortable feeling that she'd just discovered something that she hadn't expected.

Her gaze inscrutable, she quietly said, "It wasn't mine." Then she stood up, turned away, and was gone.

* * *

A WEEK LATER, I WAS sitting at our usual poker night. For once, my head wasn't in the game. *Looks like Jim might even win this round!*

I couldn't fathom it. Nora's final words kept rattling at me, and it grated that I couldn't figure out why. *Damn.* Shaking my head, I tried to put it from my thoughts, noticing that Don and Artie seemed a bit off tonight too.

"Whoo-hoo!" gushed Jim, beaming as he pulled his winnings towards him across the table. "Hey, you know our last little bet?" he continued euphorically, oblivious to anything except the coveted cash. "Well, it's given me an idea for our next one. You guys want to hear it?!"

After only the briefest of pauses, the three of us roared the exact same sentiment in powerfully determined unison:

"*No!*"

Miss Marguerite

"So, hon," leona said, a comedic note overlaying her normally casual tone, "are your soccer buddies still bugging you with the whole *Miss Marguerite* thing?"

"What?!" I chirped, surprised by my wife's question. "Why are you bringing *that* up?" Surely, that was old news by now.

"Just curious," she continued, shrugging, "I know they really wound you up about it for a long while."

"Yeah," I conceded, reluctantly. "They didn't want to let it go. It was just too funny to them. That's done with now though. Well," I added dryly, "mostly, anyway. Why?"

She paused, balancing the camper's box of canned goods and non-perishables on her hip. "Well, I know you had to take the job. We… Well, you know. We…" She was struggling to find the right words.

"I know," I said, letting her off the hook. "We needed the money." I broke out laughing at the same time she did, realising that she'd chimed in and said that last part right along with me.

"I'm just wondering if this isn't the time to quit *all* of that?" she said innocently once the laughter had died out. I wasn't fooled by the feigned casualness of the inquiry. I knew my wife better than that. Leona never spoke idly.

"Okay, Leelee, what's really going on here?" I asked, setting the fishing tackle to one side, noticing that I could still hear the kids and the dogs in the backyard. Of course, "kids" wasn't exactly the right term to use anymore. Hard to believe that they were already fourteen, sixteen, and seventeen. They were all still eager for the May long-weekend camping trip to the lake though. *Wait… Was that a rumble of thunder in the distance?*

I shook my head, dismissing the weather and refocussing on my wife. "Leona, what is it?"

She set the box down and faced me.

"Things aren't the same as when you took over Marguerite's column ten years ago. It's different now…" She paused, as if searching for words.

"Different? What do you mean?" In reality, I already knew. I just needed to hear her verify what I'd already been feeling for months.

Sighing, she dropped into the nearest camping chair, slumping back in her seat, and started talking about how I'd come to be Miss Marguerite in the first place, reminding me of the fact that I'd only taken over Marguerite Dawson's newspaper column because she'd left the paper in the lurch, giving them only three days' notice that she was done with it and retiring, which would undoubtedly hurt their readership numbers.

I nodded, smiling at the memory. "Yeah, and they had problems lining up a volunteer to fill in for a short time until they hired someone permanent."

"Volunteer?" Leona scoffed. "More like *sucker*. No one was going to step forward to be an advice guru. Nobody." Despite the fact that her column's popularity had been falling for some time, the paper had decided it was worth keeping, rather than alienating its fans.

"Well, if you recall, the money for the job was pretty good," I pointed out, catching her eye. Neither one of us had to state the obvious. With three kids—Gina in particular, needing surgeries and constant care—Leona had made the decision to stay home, which had meant one less salary coming in. But the bills had still been there, needing to be paid.

"Well," I said, trying to justify something and not knowing really why or what, "they didn't exactly hogtie me, and remember…at the time, it really *was* supposed to be temporary, just until they found someone better suited."

"Of course." She laughed humourlessly. "And ten years is temporary. Right. Actually, now that I think about it, it's actually closer to eleven years." She narrowed her eyes teasingly at me. "You've probably got that nailed down to the exact minute, don't you?"

Ignoring her last comment, I said, somewhat proudly, "It's not my fault that I ended up surprising everyone. Including myself. Who knew I'd be so good at shelling out advice?"

She smirked at that. "Probably just because, as the oldest of six kids, you're used to being a little general."

"General?" I repeated, chuckling. "As I'm more of a water and boat guy, I was thinking admiral, at least."

There was a short silence before Leona offered some further thoughts, "I can't argue with the fact that the money's been great, or even with the paper opting to keep the column's old name, despite you being heckled by everyone about being the new *Miss Marguerite*. Too risky financially and everything to change it, unless you started skewing the readership, writing stuff that she never would have."

"Yeah," I said, "and I didn't do that, though maybe I should have." The loyal readers of the original Miss Marguerite had accepted me and my advice with no issue, and by the time I realized that there was nothing temporary about the position, so had our families and friends. Staying with the extra job had seemed to work out well for everyone, and it just seemed a bit silly to bother risking changing the name of the column to *Mr. Neale* or some other such moniker.

"You have to admit though," I said, "I did spew some pretty awesome advice, if I do say so myself!"

"Most of the time," laughed Leona, grudgingly.

"Most?" I echoed with an exaggerated guffaw. "Heck, I think I've done pretty well." Remembering suddenly why we were talking about this at all, I paused, and then asked her solemnly, "So, what's the problem now?"

I pulled up another camp chair and perched myself in front of her.

"Well, we don't actually need the money so much anymore," Leona began slowly. "I'm back working, and Gina...well, Gina's doing really well now that she's a teenager, involved in sports and other activities." I smiled at this simple truth, as it was something that we'd never figured could happen for our daughter.

"Okay," I nodded seriously, "I agree with all that, but why do you suddenly think I should quit?"

She stared at me, clear-eyed, and gave me a small, knowing smile. "I think you know...It's because of everything. Because of the way things are nowadays. You know."

I did know and almost hated to admit it. She was right, but I didn't think I was quite ready to acknowledge such defeat. "Okay, what are we talking about, really?" I asked, realising that my tone was making the question sound like an interrogation. Regardless, I needed to hear it. Out loud.

"You know as well as I do, Neale." She sighed. "It's people. The world. Everything. It's all different. It's like it's crept up on us, but really, it hasn't. We just weren't paying attention."

Leona was so astute, and pretty darn fantastic at figuring out people...and stuff in general, really. She should have finished her psychology degree. Still could. But I needed to find a different moment to discuss that with her.

I leaned over and took her hands in mine. "Okay, so then what? Spell it out for me," I pressed in a wheedling tone.

She started speaking slowly, sort of feeling her way along. "Well, back then, readers wrote in physically, asking things like, 'Do you think my husband is cheating on me?' Or 'What should I really be telling my mother-in-law about our married life?' Or even 'What can I do now that my best friend doesn't want to be friends anymore?' People-based questions...about life, family, kids...But now..."

"Now?" I said softly, urging her to go on, even as I heard that distant rumble again, a bit louder now. *Okay, that was definitely thunder. Why does it always have to rain on the May long weekend?!*

Leona's brow was furrowed, though she seemed oblivious to the darkening skies. "Well, now the questions are just tossed effortlessly into a general social-media swirl. Anything from 'How can I stop my kids doing drugs?' to 'Why are they still dumping raw sewage into the ocean?' and 'When are they going to ban disposable diapers?' Oh, and by the way," she said then, raising a finger skyward for emphasis, "that last one is kind of the sacred elephant in the room and never going to happen," she finished cynically.

I'd thought she was finished, but she was only warming up. She suddenly sat bolt upright in her camp chair and added passionately, "But it isn't just the controversial questions, Neale. That's only *half* the equation. Any answers given are seldom ever just accepted at face value. They're literally scrutinized. Dissected. Every word. Any responses harkening to common sense, common courtesy, or heaven forbid, customer service, are no longer acceptable. Too old school, apparently, and regularly empaled and obliterated from discussion. It's like this new techy world has pitched all that by the wayside. This *isn't* the 'old days,'" she said, with air quotes, "and so you can't just *give advice* like in the 'old days.'

"Everything has to be sanitized first," she continued. "If one wrong word is said or written by *anyone*, the social-vilification process begins. You know that better than most, Neale. The endless hours you put in to ensure that not even a single word can be mis-construed and insult, traumatize, or offend anyone. You know it. I know it. I've seen the worry and the stress it puts on you, and all the extra editing time you put in so that you won't—fingers crossed—be misunderstood, and then maligned. Remember that column you wrote last year that got you persecuted for months?" she asked rhe-torically, then stopped, sighing in resignation.

I nodded, remembering the column in question all too clearly, with a certain bitterness. It had literally taken several weeks for the heat to even start to settle down. "Okay, so just say I do decide to quit. What then?"

"What do you mean?" she asked quizzically, leaning towards me.

"Well, obviously, the extra money will be gone, for one thing. I'll be back to regular reporting, which is also a lot different than it was ten years ago, though it's been chiseled at in its own special way."

"Nothing is what it used to be," she added, sadness entering her voice. "The world's changing, Neale. And I don't know that we're the type of people to change with it, at least not in the way it wants us to."

I suspected she was right. We were in our forties now, and though I hate to say it, more or less settled in our ways. We believed in a certain code of conduct for ourselves, our kids, and from society at large. A lot of that was eroding around us.

She wasn't done and took my hands in hers as she continued. "Neale...I just worry that eventually—and it could literally be any day now—you'll print something that the wrong person will find randomly unsuitable, and your reputation will be utterly destroyed this time." She stopped then, apparently sensing that she might have said too much.

"You're right," I conceded without reservation because it was just the truth.

Leona stared as if she couldn't quite believe what she was hearing and was afraid to get her hopes up. "You mean you'll *actually* consider the possibility of quitting the column?" Her tone was incredulous. "Really?"

I couldn't help being a little surprised by her reaction. Leona was never impulsive in her decision making, so this was obviously something that had been stirring around in her cranium for quite some time.

"Okay," I said, knowing full well that now that this topic was out there between the two of us, there was no way it could be returned to Pandora's Box. Something was definitely going to have to change.

I gave her a look. "I can see that you've been stewing about this for a bit, Leelee." Leona's eyebrows raised in surprise, which made me smile. "Yes, I *do* know you *that* well," I said, giving her hands a gentle squeeze and changing tactics. "And I meant it when I said that you were right. This isn't just about us. It's about the kids too."

"Yeah, it is," she agreed, her eyes searching mine. "I don't like what this family is becoming, almost disappearing into itself for fear of appearing as something we're not. We both know that all of us are in the public eye simply because of what you do. You talk to people, so to speak, through the written word, but I hear stuff from those same people directly. Friends. My parents even. And the kids do too. They get hassled by the kids at school from time to time about things you've written, and sometimes even by other parents. Almost like an inquisition."

"Inquisition?" I repeated, startled. No. Not startled. It was more than that. I was alarmed. Fearful. It had honestly never occurred to me that the kids were facing any kind of backlash because of my job.

Her eyes widened at seeing my reaction. "You really didn't have any idea, did you?" She looked genuinely astounded.

Leona gently pulled her hands from within mine, and folded mine inside her own instead. "I'm sorry, Neale, but I made sure they came to me whenever they had any problems," she said tenderly. "I thought it better for the kids and I to manage the issue without bothering you." She shrugged slightly. "I have to admit that I was wrong about that."

"You...and the kids..." I mumbled, dumbstruck. A form of delayed shock hit me then, followed almost instantly by a shot of anger. "I'm done," I said with an unequivocal decisiveness that startled even Leona. "I'm quitting the column."

"Neale," she began, and then fell back in her chair with the sudden awareness that the lid of Pandora's box had swung open even wider. "I hadn't meant for you to make an instant decision. I..." At a loss for words, she let her voice trail off even as her gaze begged for understanding.

"It isn't," I said with a bold and honest stare. "I think I just needed some kind of final shot between the eyes to cement the deal. Stuff I've already sensed. That's all. *Truly.*"

Leona slouched still deeper into her chair like a deflated balloon. "I know you, Neale. You usually stumble and hesitate before you make a decision on anything major. Seriously...Are you sure you're ready for this, or did I just push you into the deep end without your floaties?"

She scanned my face, a small smile starting in her eyes at whatever she saw there before it finally reached the corners of her mouth and tugged them upwards. She sat up a bit straighter, and then leaned forward a bit as if to examine me. After a moment's consideration, she shook her head in amazement. "You *are* ready, aren't you? This is really it?"

"It really is. And right now, too," I said. I felt an invisible weight start sliding off my shoulders.

"You can't just quit like *that,*" she said, snapping her fingers emphatically as if to wake me up. "The paper could totally fire you,

Neale, and that includes your regular reporting job too. All of it could be instantly gone. You *do* realize that possibility, don't you?" she pressed, sharply externalizing the probable unintended consequences. When I didn't respond immediately, lost in thought, she snapped her fingers again. "Neale, are you listening? Are you *really* sure about this?"

"Yes, I am," I said, my sudden resolve jarring even to me. I could see by the sudden fear in her eyes that the small (though catastrophizing) thought she'd just verbalized had instantly erupted into something with much larger and further-reaching implications for our future.

"Leelee, this is me," I said quietly, leaning closer. "This is *us*. Our family and the value we all place on upholding certain principles. This last year has been hell. I somehow hadn't realized it extended beyond me, but that stops now. Do you hear? This is not going to continue. In all honesty, my confidence in the column has been gone for a while now, and I've been mostly treading water, trying not to drown. Maybe it all started last year with that incident, but I think it's been festering for even longer than that. There's a societal shift out there, in so many different arenas, but I'm not about to cave when it comes to my beliefs. *Our* beliefs."

I squeezed her hands again. "I used to feel that I had some sort of helpful influence, but I've come to slowly realize that whatever sway I once held just isn't there anymore. Now the stinging criticism is almost constant, just hovering around me, ready to pounce if I make a single mistake. And anyway, lately I've just felt the strongest desire to do something else entirely. Anything, really. Sounds crazy, right?"

This time it was my wife who provided the reassurance of a gentle hand squeeze as I continued. "Writing that column, I've been feeling beyond vulnerable for longer than I care to admit. So truly, with absolute seriousness, I can say that I just don't want to do it anymore." I paused, suddenly feeling exhausted. "I can't," I added with a finality to my voice that shocked me, even as it solidified my conviction that this was the only right decision I could make.

"Okay, then," she said, her smile widening. "We'll *make* it work."

"Make what work?" echoed Max, rounding the corner of the house, gangly, inquisitive, and only months away from becoming an adult. "Hey, buddy," I ribbed good-naturedly, avoiding a direct response. "Perfect timing! Where are your brother and sister? You guys can help finish loading the camper. The lake's waiting!"

"Aw, come on, Dad," he lamented sourly, glancing at the black clouds rolling in. "It's going to rain any second."

"It's *not* going to rain!" I yelped good-naturedly, jumping up with renewed fervor, a long-dormant elation surging through me at last. "Joey, Gina, come over here!" I yelled towards the backyard.

Almost immediately, several large droplets splattered down amidst a brilliant lightning display that splintered the sky, with a bellowing roll of thunder close on its heels.

"See, Dad? I told you!" Max gloated, almost jubilantly.

Two racing black labs bolted around the corner of the house then, with Gina and Joey sprinting close behind, just as the downpour began in earnest.

"Grab something!" I shouted.

Loading up the rest of our stuff took less than a minute. Once everything had been liberally chucked through the open camper door, we hurled ourselves inside as well. The dogs were already curled up, comfortably dry, beneath the table, as Leona, the kids, and I stood there, panting, dripping, and listening to the rain that was drumming rhythmically on the camper's metal roof.

"Um…Dad?" Max turned to look at me with humour twinkling in his eyes. "I can't say for sure, but I think it might just rain this weekend after all."

The Peacock Hat

THURSDAY, 14 APRIL 1938, FRANKFURT
HAUPTBAHNHOF (MAIN TRAIN STATION)

JAMMING THE UNOPENED CIGARETTE POUCH into my coat pocket, I tried concentrating on something else as I set my suitcase down and checked the station clock suspended between *Gleis* 9 and *Gleis* 10. It was 10:22 a.m.

I had a sudden sinking feeling that I was making a huge mistake. *I must be. Everyone says so,* I reminded myself. *Are they right? How hard would it be to get my job back?* Fighting an intense desire to simply pick up my bag and go home, I took a deep breath and focused on the crowded platform.

There was the usual allotment of tradesmen and day labourers with their work-worn hands stuffed into the pockets of stained trousers. Knitted hats and battered fedoras were pulled low over jaded stares and exhausted faces.

Two days ago, that had been me.

I nodded at the few of them I recognized. Got some nods back. None here that I knew well. I had thought there might be. A last farewell. Best wishes. Like that.

No surprise that my family wasn't here, having told me only to "See sense." From the first announcement of my intentions, there was only derision. I had anticipated an initial shock over my declaration that I was moving away. What I hadn't expected was the continued ridicule. A constant barrage of advice that I should be well satisfied I had a job. *"Many don't."* That was the constant reminder. It was time to get married. Start a family. But leaving the country? *"To Canada? Are you crazy?"* It rarely let up. I sighed. My jaw clenching, I knew that I wasn't going home. To admit a blunder? To listen to their triumph? No!

More disappointing than the fact that no family was here, there was no one from my former work crew either. *Probably at a job,* I convinced myself, trying to put sudden nostalgia aside. *Time to look forward.*

Again, I allowed my eyes to wander over the busy platform. Intermingling amongst the workers were excited scatterings of children and youth in white shirts and school uniforms, carrying dangling book bags. Many families of varying sizes too. Everyone appeared to be taking early advantage of the upcoming long weekend. I couldn't help but smile at one cajoling mother gently herding her brood of six before her, the family's patriarch staunchly steering the queue.

Everything *seemed* normal, and yet…I frowned. There was a palpable tension. It was too quiet. Tomorrow's Good Friday, a solemn day of prayer, could account for some of it. However, with the anticipation of a festive Easter Sunday, I knew that I should be witnessing some animated chatter, banter, and relaxed camaraderie, instead of hushed whispers amidst covert glances. Even the children's normally shrill and spirited babble echoed on a lower octave. I tensed, inhaling hard, suddenly observing what I had failed to comprehend until now. A measured exhalation followed.

Militär…Soldaten.

Military…Soldiers. Standing in knotted clusters of two and three. The majority of whom were outfitted in the basic garb of army regulars. Here and there were also high-ranking officials, their distinctive insignia setting them unquestionably apart. And above. Then I remembered. There was a morning train to Berlin.

My throat constricted.

Last week's jarring street search was still fresh in my memory. It had been more a combative inquisition, really. *"You're not German,"* the soldiers had sneered, scoffing at my family name. It didn't matter that my documents confirmed I was German-born. No sense explaining where the town of Herne was located. They weren't interested. *"Immigrant,"* they'd snorted, arrogantly certain my documents were skewed. They weren't. Everything was genuine. Nonetheless, I had been afraid. That same terror coursed through me now.

I was sharply jostled from behind and nearly knocked off my feet. "Ummph," I grunted.

Just as I was about to spin around and give a stinging retort, I felt an urgent tug on my opposing sleeve. Instinctively, I turned in that direction. A woman's eyes flashed a caution. Rotating slowly back the other way, I was just in time to witness the military officer who'd bumped me striding boldly past, humanity parting hurriedly for him and his two-man escort.

I turned back to the woman. "Thank you," I murmured. She nodded, her gaze remaining vigilantly alert.

At that moment, it was all I could do not to sprint for the Köln Express that I knew was idling on *Gleis* 8. Anything to get away! It was scheduled to depart shortly, awaiting only a transfer of passengers arriving from München on *Gleis* 10. The München train would leave Frankfurt at 10:40 on its scheduled run to Hamburg Hauptbahnhof. *With me on board!* I thought happily.

Once in Hamburg, the Port of Hamburg would be an easy walk. A couple of kilometres only. I thought suddenly of the official papers tucked snugly inside the lining of my vest, resisting the urge to ensure that they were still secure. I rechecked the time. It was 10:26.

I forced myself to remain calm. *Only a few minutes more,* I kept repeating silently. Forcing my gaze away from the clock, I turned back to the crowd.

A hint of colour caught my eye. A woman's hat. Brilliant blue like a peacock, making me remember a certain favourite children's book. Only then did I notice the woman beneath the hat. In her twenties, perhaps. Frail. No, not that. Something else. Fearful. Yes, afraid.

His back partially to me, a man was speaking to her. His familiarity suggested it could only be her husband. I was too far away to hear words, but his intimidating stance suggested force. Anger. She cowered, visibly attempting to shrink away from him. It was then I noticed the boy. No older than two or three. Clearly frightened, he pressed himself tightly against her.

Suddenly and without warning, the man brutally struck the boy's face, flinging his head to one side. The child reacted with a piercing howl, immediately subsiding to a whimper as the man raised his hand to strike again. The woman grabbed the boy, snatching him up and shielding him securely against her.

Instantly horrified, I unconsciously stepped forward, then froze at the flash of military crests on the man's uniform. My fists clenched, but I moved no further. No one intervened. Most turned aside, pretending not to see.

Shouting one final time, the man spun about. For an instant, I saw his face, wild fury contorting his features. He stomped angrily out of sight, the crowd parting swiftly before him.

I did something then that I will never be able to fully explain. My gaze locking on the peacock hat, I unbuttoned the top pocket inside my coat. Fingering the bills inside, I counted some out, rolling them firmly inside my palm. My fist closed around them. Without a further thought, I stepped forward, my eyes still on the hat and the woman cradling her son, rocking him tenderly.

I walked fast. Time was short. Her husband could return at any moment. As soon as I reached her, I said, "Excuse me. Please."

She raised her head in alarm.

"Excuse me," I repeated, and then added quickly, "I can help you, but there isn't much time."

"What…?" she began, glancing at me in confusion and dismay.

"I can help," I repeated, "but we have to hurry."

I moved closer. Unconsciously, she stepped back, more perplexed than afraid. Though there were people everywhere, I felt certain no one was paying attention. Many intentionally. It was clear none wanted to be involved.

"The Köln Express on *Gleis* 8 is departing in a few moments. I can give you some money…enough to get you and your son to Köln…*To get away,*" I stressed, sensing that I wasn't getting through to her. I indicated the currency inside my closed hand.

She continued to stare as if I'd lost my wits.

"Do you *want* to get away?" I asked urgently. Time was fleeting. The train was due to leave. "I have money. Take it," I gestured.

She backed away, glancing anxiously around. "What are you doing?" she asked, truly confused.

"I am trying to help you," I stated clearly. "Take the money and get on the Express. It goes directly to Köln. Once you get there, go to the Dom. You know the *Kölner Dom*, don't you? The cathedral with the two spires?" I was speaking rapidly, trying to think of everything. "Ask for Father Benedict. Do you hear? Father Benedict. He will help you. Tell him that Stefan sent you. Stefan, the stone mason. Just say that. He'll understand. Can you remember? Are you listening?" I questioned, my voice rising, suddenly panicked that she hadn't heard a word.

"Stefan," she repeated, nodding vaguely, her face blank. Suddenly, the boy stirred and turned his head, staring wordlessly at me. A large red welt marked his cheek.

"You have one minute," I stressed emphatically. "That's all before the train leaves." In truth, I didn't know exactly how long. All I recognized was that it was soon, hearing a whistle heralding the arrival of the train from München.

I glanced at her son, innocently looking back at me. "Do it for the boy," I said passionately.

Dazed, she looked at the child, and then back at me. Her gaze cleared. She nodded, holding out her hand. I pressed the bills into it, and her fingers folded around them.

"Walk quickly. Don't run," I urged before adding, "Hide the hat." At her puzzled look, I said, "Too visible. Now go, and don't look back!"

"Thank you…thank you," she mouthed silently, her eyes filling with tears. She wrenched off the hat and picked up a small valise from the platform. Still clutching her son in her arms, she walked swiftly away. A second later, she was swallowed up by the crowd.

I suddenly remembered my own suitcase and let out a desolate sigh. *Everything I own is in that bag,* I despaired. Dejected and without hope, I rushed back to where I had been standing. With a dumbfounded look, I saw it sitting exactly where I had left it!

"You were busy. We watched over it for you," said an older man standing nearby. "I'm Oleg. This is Frederic." His head tilted towards a younger man.

A huge smile lit my face. "Stefan," I said, offering my name as utter relief flooded through me. I stretched out my hand, and he folded his calloused one around mine. Then I received a second handshake from Frederic. "Thank you so much."

Hearing a whistle in the distance, I suddenly wondered if the woman had made it to the train on time.

As if reading my thoughts, Oleg stated matter-of-factly, "She's safely on board."

Reality and fear hit suddenly at the same time, and I started trembling. If they had seen my actions, so had others!

"He's back," hissed Frederic quietly. He pushed me abruptly out of sight behind him and Oleg.

"Lower your head. Stay quiet," Oleg warned.

I forced myself not to look as angry tones echoed nearby. Commands shouted. Paralyzed with fear, I stood frozen.

"Hamburg, right?" asked Oleg in a whisper.

"Yes," I answered, my heart pounding.

"Get on now! The train is almost finished boarding. Go!" he ordered sternly.

Awaking from my stupor and giving him a short nod, I grabbed my bag and joined the last few stragglers. I forced myself not to look around even as I heard more orders being called out amidst a heated uproar. Once inside the third-class carriage, I slunk low in a back corner seat, praying feverishly that the train would soon be underway.

It felt an eternity before the whistle echoed, though it was probably little more than a minute. Only as the train lurched forward slowly gathering steam did I dare risk a look towards the platform. There was no Oleg. No Frederic. And more importantly, no military!

I leaned back and released a huge pent-up breath. As I reached inside my coat to refasten the buttons of the inner pocket, I realized that my hands were trembling, and suddenly, I couldn't stop shaking. Whatever had possessed me to do that? Deep down, of course, I knew. There was no mystery. Senseless brutality was not something I could easily dismiss. The real question was how I'd garnered the courage to act.

A bizarre thought suddenly crossed my mind: *My last experiences in this country of my birth have all been with strangers, and from this moment on, that's all there ever will be: strangers.*

I leaned back and idly stuffed my hands in my pockets, coming up against the cigarette pouch. I had forgotten all about it! *Maybe it isn't going to be as hard to quit smoking as I thought.* I found myself smiling.

Staring out of the window, I tried to imagine what Canada would be like. I knew it was large, but what I was yet to discover was how truly inadequate that word would turn out to be.

Once A Pawn

"WHAT DO YOU THINK MY Thursday yoga classes would say if they knew I'd cut today's sessions because I'd received a surprise invitation from action hero Alastair Deacon and been flown to his movie set?" I said, grinning.

Laughing, Alastair shook his head. "No idea, but I'm pretty sure I can guess *your* reaction if I said that Helen Mirren was here."

"Oh my God, is she?!" I gushed and actually swung my gaze around the RV as if she might magically pop up somewhere.

Alastair chuckled.

"Oh, Buddy," I huffed, good-naturedly, forgetting what a prankster he used to be. "Seriously, it was great to hear from you, but I can't help wondering why. It's been years, and then suddenly, out of the blue, you invite me to see you. Why?" I asked soberly, suddenly worried that he had dire news to share. "Are you okay?"

"You know, you're the only person who's ever called me buddy," he said gently. "And I'm fine. Now, don't think I can't read you, Della. I know you're dying to ask about Keeley, but as much as social media tries to run it otherwise, we're still together and doing just fine!"

A warm glow settled over me. Literally everything I knew about Alastair now had been gleaned through the negligible information the media managed to scrape together about his closely guarded personal life. He still had no social-media presence whatsoever!

I said nothing more. Cradling my cup, I waited.

"I need to ask you to do something for me," he said finally. He stood up and walked to the RV's massive window, staring out at the distant Rockies. I thought I detected a certain unease, but a second later, it was gone, convincing me I'd been mistaken.

"Okay," I answered. "What do you need?"

For Buddy, I would do almost anything, but I was puzzled. No doubt, he had a range of people who could get all manner of stuff done for him. So, why me?

He turned around. "Do you remember the bad closet?" he asked, staring at me intently.

I was startled. My throat constricted. "Yeah."

The summer I'd turned ten, there had been a major shakeup at social services, resulting in foster kids being arbitrarily shuffled around. The new house I'd been sent to was bigger, with tougher kids and more of them. It operated on the same principle as the previous one though: *"Do as you're told."* Period. I had been in the system long enough by then and learned a couple of additional survival tactics: Stay invisible, and don't ask questions.

Right from the get-go, a couple of the girls had picked up on the fact that I would be an easy target. I'd tried to stay out of their way, but they'd tormented me for days. Finally, they'd gotten me alone. Trapped in a corner of the backyard. Suddenly, an older kid turned up, and after few terse words from him, they scattered. (I later learned that they had planned to soak me with the garden hose, followed by a flour shower.)

This must be the top dog, I'd reasoned. My fear doubling, I'd wondered what he had in store for me, but all he'd said to me was *"Don't let them get to you, Della. Alright?"*

I'd mustered a nod, shocked that he even knew my name. "Thanks, buddy," I'd managed to croak out as he walked away. With his now famous smile, he'd given me a mock salute, and then disappeared around the corner of the house. That's how he had come into my life, and I'd liked to think of him as my secret older brother.

Buddy had his own set of rules, though, some of which did not always jive with the powers in charge. More than once, he'd ended up in the "bad closet."

First off, it wasn't actually a closet. It was the main-floor portion of a curved staircase that had been boarded shut at the second floor, preventing access to or from that section of the house. A door had been installed at its bottom, sealing in the tiny landing and unusable stairs. Little more than a niche, really. This was where the *bad* kids ended up, those kids who'd decided that the house rules weren't for them. Someone had named it the bad closet. The name stuck.

I'd smugly known that I would never end up in there. Then one night, our supper had been lentil soup. I'd stared at that bowl of pond scum for I don't know how long. Couldn't push in even a single spoonful. Going to bed hungry, I'd woken up famished in the middle of the night. The house was so quiet that I'd taken a chance and gone downstairs. One of the first rules drilled into us kids was that the kitchen was off-limits. And the fridge a definite, rock-solid no go. Food was doled out, and we got what we got.

I hesitated the barest of seconds, then opened the refrigerator door. The interior light came on, and the first thing I spied was a bowl of raspberries. I had planned to just eat a few, but I was so hungry that I'd started gobbling. Then the main kitchen light had snapped on, and I was grabbed in a fistful of hair and basically dragged away, obscene expletives hammering at me the whole time. I knew what was going to happen and was powerless to stop it!

One hard push, and I was inside the closet. The door was flung shut and its heavy bolt slid across. A padlock clicked. It was pitch black, the nearly airless space reeking of sweat and urine. My jailer's footsteps retreated then, and total silence closed in. Without warning, I upchucked a cup's worth of raspberries.

"I bought the house, Della," Buddy said, interrupting my reverie.

"What? Why?" I was shocked.

He shrugged and sighed, plopping himself into a sofa chair. "Just being stupid, really. Had a few drinks one night and started thinking too much. Remembering stuff. You know what I mean." He gave me a look.

I nodded. I'd had moments like that too.

"Well, I was going to have it ripped down. As a sort of closure, I guess. To finally put those years behind me. Life got busy though, and I didn't get around to it…And, well, it turns out that now I can't."

"Why not? It's yours, isn't it?"

"The short answer is yes. I bought and paid for it. Even got renters in there. But a few weeks back, the town designated it a heritage site. Can you believe it? They sent a letter explaining. Some important immigrant apparently settled there umpteen years ago. He started out as a trapper, then opened some kind of shop while also building that house. The town kind of grew from that. Well, long story short, council decided to have it restored. There's a huge ceremony next year for the anniversary, and the plan is to have it finished by then. From what the letter said, restoration is scheduled to start pretty quick."

I didn't quite know what to say. What was the problem? And what did any of it actually have to do with me. "Are they expecting you to pay for it?"

"Hell, no." He laughed. "There's some sort of fund for that type of thing. The government is even tossing a few bucks at it. And anyway, nobody knows it's me who owns it. Shows up as a numbered company, just like a couple other properties I have. Keeps everything at a bit of a distance." He didn't have to say more. Buddy had always been secretive.

"Where do I come in?" I suddenly had to know.

Looking directly at me, he said, "I need something from there that I left behind. Once they start ripping up walls and stuff, it's bound to show up, and for obvious reasons, I can't just go get it myself." He sighed. "I know I should have dealt with this long ago. I just...Well, I didn't, and..." He was struggling with what to say and how to say it. This was a side of Buddy I didn't know at all. His soft underbelly, if you will.

I leaned over and touched his arm. "Just tell me, and I'll get it. No questions. Okay?"

✳ ✳ ✳

THE FLIGHT WENT SMOOTHLY, THOUGH a computer glitch had lost my car rental. Luckily, I had a hard copy of the agreement and received an upgrade as a gesture of good will. Relishing the SUV's luxury drive, I was sorry when it reached its end. Buildings came into sight as I made the final turn, dipping into the valley, the first reminder that I'd promised myself to never come back here.

Oh, well, I thought, sighing.

I hadn't eaten since scarfing down a muffin at the airport Tim Hortons, so I took a left and pulled into the local diner. Still popular, judging by the number of vehicles parked outside. A few things had changed though. The exterior's paint job had gone from bleached purple to vibrant lime. It even had new windows and paved parking now.

Hot summer air slammed me as I exited the vehicle. A minute later, I entered the café's coolness. That was something else new: air conditioning. The interior hadn't really changed and still smelled the same, though I suppose that fast-food odours are the same no matter where you are. Treating myself to a huge order of fries and large iced tea, I slid into a vacant booth at the back. It turned out to be the best spot to observe foot traffic, as well as the drive-through. There were substantially more orders from outside than in, and thankfully, no familiar faces.

The fries were great. Lots of greasy goodness. Involuntarily, I sucked in my gut, wondering how much harder of a workout I would have to put in next week.

Afterwards, I drove around, though only for a bit—just because. Everything seemed slightly different, yet the same. A few minutes of that was enough. I had work to do.

I'd saved the house for last. Parking across the street, I slowly assessed the changes as I walked over. It had always stood in a rather peculiar area of town. Basically, swallowed inside a light industrial zone. Two metal shops to the south and a trucking firm next door.

The stark white stucco I remembered was now muck brown. Only one teetering side remained of the spacious, wrap-around veranda where us kids liked to chase one another. All grass was gone. The front was a rutted parking space. From what I could see of the back, it had been relegated to a kind of graveyard for derelict vehicles and worn-out machinery.

No unwanted memories cropped up, for which I was grateful.

Buddy had been right that restorations were planned. What he hadn't been so right about was how soon. Off to the side, heavy chain link and barbed wire belted in all manner of building materials. The timing of my visit was pretty tight.

A giant handmade sign stating "Books and Stuff" was stuck in a side window near the front entrance. A crisscross banner advertising "Moving Out Sale" had been plastered on top of it, obliterating some of the first sign's lettering. Walking closer, I noticed a small note crammed into a crevice of the door frame. "Back at one," it read. Being that it was now coming on two o'clock, it made me wonder if it was actually closed for the rest of the day.

This sucks, I thought, wondering what to do.

Just as I was trying to figure it out, a man and woman came along down the back alleyway. Both appeared to be in their thirties, and I couldn't help but notice the woman's barely-there jean shorts. *Good legs, though,* I had to admit. Paying me no mind, they walked straight towards the rear of the building.

"Excuse me!" I called, raising my voice slightly to carry the distance. "Do you know if the bookstore is open today?"

"Should be," answered the man, his cap sporting a Yankees logo. "Bruce probably had to run some errands. We live upstairs," he ended. With that comment, they went inside and left me standing there.

So much for small-town hospitality, I thought, somewhat annoyed and not sure why.

I was just about to go back to my airconditioned vehicle when a battered pickup pulled in. The truck's vintage was uncertain, but it had definitely seen better times. Its front bumper was a wooden beam that had been strapped on with ropes and bungee cords. Rusted side panels shook mightily as the truck bounced in and then out of a massive pothole before sputtering to a stuttering stop. Faded script on the door panel extolled the virtues of "Jake's Masonry – No Job Too Small."

A guy about fifty years old, sporting a short ponytail, ripped t-shirt, and baggy sweatpants, stepped out of the vehicle. Hoisting a flat of twenty-four canned Labatt's Blue from the seat, he kicked the door shut and wobbled towards me. The beer was ice cold, as evidenced by glistening condensation visible through the plastic wrap.

"Hi," I said with a smile as he neared the shop. "Are you Bruce?"

He looked in my direction and kind of ogled me. That hadn't happened in a while, and I wasn't sure what to do, so I just ignored it.

He nodded, his single earring stud dancing brilliantly in the sunlight. "The shop will be open in a second. Was just picking up a few provisions for the weekend." Depositing the beer by the door, he sauntered to the back of the truck, dropped a creaking tailgate, and wrenched out a bulky cooler.

I thought I might as well hurry things along and stepped over to give him a hand, scooping up a couple of overfull plastic grocery bags. Hot-dog buns, marshmallows, chips, pretzels, and the like. The usual healthy summer-meal choices.

"A few of us are having a barbeque," he offered by way of explanation. The weighty cooler landed on the stoop, with an "oomph" from him. Tugging a hefty keyring from his sweats, he inserted one into the lock and opened the door. "After you."

I stepped into my past and recognized nothing.

Other than a narrow pathway, every available fragment of space was crammed with uneven stacks of books, boxes, knick-knacks, pieces of furniture, and heaven knows what else. *Like a thrift store on crack*, I thought wildly.

"Help yourself," he offered, his eyes sweeping the room. I imagined him taking visual inventory in the event I decided to abscond with some valuable artifact. I almost laughed. *Almost.*

As Bruce busied himself with storing the beer in a fridge in the room beyond, I looked around. A shudder passed through me as my eyes landed on the bad closet. The door was gone, its hinges the only remaining evidence of its previous existence.

Bruce returned just as I walked over and peered into the opening. Minus the door, it wasn't so scary. Couldn't actually see much though. It was plumb chock-a-block full. Piles of books and boxes. And boxes and books. My heart sank. How was I ever going to get in there? Feigning an interest in everything inside, my mind was racing. What to do?

"What time do you close?" I asked nonchalantly, hoping maybe he would just go away in the back and I could quickly do what I came here for. If all else failed, there was a backup plan, though I hesitated to use it: returning later once Bruce had gone home and using the key that Buddy had given me to gain entry. He'd said it was an old one and admitted, with a laugh, that *"maybe"* the locks had been changed since then. Of course, I didn't particularly like this option. No matter how I might try to justify it to myself, it would still be breaking in.

"Take your time," he said then. Snapping the tab on a beer can, he sucked back its contents greedily.

"Thanks," I said, longing suddenly for a cold one too. *He could have offered me one.* Small towns had definitely changed. *For God's sake, Della,* I told myself. *Get a grip!*

My mind was trying to invent some manner of easily disassembling the towers inside the tiny alcove without attracting undue attention. After all, there were boxes everywhere much more accessible that I could be checking into. *How to get them gone,* I wondered. Then I saw something.

At the back corner, buried beneath the deluge, I spied the edge of a small desk. Just a desk. Nothing special. But I decided to turn it into something extraordinary.

"Oh, that's a lovely desk you've got in there!" I acclaimed loudly, as if it was the most astonishing item I had ever seen. "Is it for sale too?" I inquired in such a heady tone that there was no way he could ignore my eagerness. The first rule of bartering was to never express noticeable enthusiasm as the customer. On this occasion, though, I wanted to break that rule as noticeably as possible.

He stomped over, squinted inside, and said brusquely, "Well, not sure about that." I knew he was attempting to figure out how much he could wrangle out of me for it.

"It's *exactly* what I've been looking for!" I raved.

"Well, in that case," he began, stepping forward and attempting to wade into the opening, "maybe I can get a few things sorted for you to have a better look."

That's the *last* thing I wanted! In an effort to steer his gallantry away from the area, I casually volunteered my services. "Listen, I can see you're busy, so I don't mind doing it myself. Besides," I said as my gaze landed on a hard-cover Jane Austen, "there are a couple of other things in there that look interesting too."

Satisfied that I seemed a genuine customer, he nodded. "Well, have at it, then." With that, he turned and made his way through the clutter, following a narrow path to the kitchen, and more importantly, out of sight.

Settling down my shoulder bag near the closet's entrance, I got to work. I was sweating in no time and wishing for air conditioning. *You work out nearly every day, girl,* I scolded myself. *Quit being such a baby!* Hunkering down, I pulled out box after box.

Suddenly, an overpowering aroma of sweat, urine, and vomit arose in my memory, forcing me to swallow hard against the bile rising in my throat. Briefly closing my eyes, I forced a few deep breaths, the steady rhythm settling my nerves.

Sucking my water bottle dry, I called out to Bruce, begging for a refill. A few minutes later, when he returned to my side with its replacement, it was accompanied by a surprising companion: an icy Labatt's Blue!

"Thanks!" I grinned foolishly. Breaking open the tab, I took a couple of deep swigs, the resultant headiness buffering the abrupt disquiet of stirring memories.

Eventually, the box columns outside the alcove grew and the bottom stairs became accessible. Ensuring that Bruce was nowhere around, I followed Buddy's directions: *"Just run your fingers lightly down the edge of the first step's face, right where it joins the wall."* I did as I'd been told and felt the slight indent he'd mentioned. Inserting the tip of my finger into the crease, I pulled the board gingerly towards me. With a faint creak, it fell forward. Inside the space sat the box Buddy had described. It was a battered little metal chest with key lock and carry handle.

All this fuss just for this? I shook my head. As I pulled it towards me though, its robust weight surprised me. Hastily swiping a layer of dust from its surface, I stuffed it in my bag. Reinserting the board, I released a shaky breath.

Done!

✳   ✳   ✳

WHEN I FINALLY DROVE AWAY, I shook my head as I berated myself. "You're an idiot," I said aloud as a quick glance in my rearview reflected the legs of the upended desk, now resting comfortably in the back of my rental. After all the hoopla I'd made about how perfect it was, I simply hadn't had the heart to tell Bruce that I had changed my mind. Instead, I convinced myself that seeing Bruce beaming would somehow be worth the price I'd paid.

As soon as I arrived back in the city, I settled the desk inside the donation bin of the first Goodwill I could find. That left only the coveted Jane Austen hard cover and the metal box, both of which were sharing space in the front passenger seat.

Upon reaching the airport, I stuffed the box into my small roller bag, deciding to check the bag instead of retaining it as a carry-on. My reasoning was simple: As I had no idea of the box's contents, airport security might determine that whatever was in there wasn't suitable for cabin travel.

Sipping a coffee as I awaited boarding, I pulled out my mobile. Only then did I notice that I had inadvertently disengaged the phone's ringtone. I had wondered why it had been so silent all day and was surprised at the number of calls I'd missed. A second glance showed that the majority were from Buddy!

A guy who had never once contacted me in all these years had now sent me over a dozen messages! And all because of a stupid box!

"What the hell?" I mumbled aloud, ready to immediately call to let him know that everything was okay. Then something popped into my head: a silly nickname from back in the day.

"Del-Ex," Hugh had laughed. *"Hey, Della, how do you like that? My friend Alastair manages to get himself his own personal Delivery Express system: Del-Ex. Get it, Dell-ah? All he has to do is snap his fingers, and there you are, shadow girl, ready to do whatever mindless task he wants done!"* He'd then laughed some more.

I hadn't found it funny. It had hurt. *And it isn't true!* I'd told myself.

Buddy had disappeared from the foster home just before he'd turned eighteen. No warning or goodbyes. Not even a note or a phone call later to say that he was okay. The only brother I'd ever had was gone, and I was heartbroken for a long time.

Years later, once his on-screen fame took off, I'd actually been happy for him. By then, my hurt and anger had dulled, and I was working on my own life. In a silly kind of way, seeing him on-screen had made it feel like my brother was finally back.

And what do I do the first instant he contacts me? Yep. I allowed myself to get sucked right back in, didn't I? Oohing and aahing at his movie set. Del-Ex again, just like Hugh said. And all because of a bloody stupid box!

Angry now, I stuffed the phone back in my purse.

By the time I got home, I had calmed down, having thought it all through. Simple, really. Buddy had sent me because he'd thought I would do exactly as I was told. The Della he remembered always had, after all. He'd somehow forgotten that I was no longer that little girl.

Suddenly, I was curious what had been worth all the bother and decided to open the box. A small screwdriver was all it took. Lifting the lid, I was momentarily stunned. It was filled with coins! *All this subterfuge for pocket change?* I thought incredulously.

A closer look told me these weren't just regular coins. Some were old. Others heavy. A few foreign. They looked valuable. There was no way these had ever belonged to Buddy.

Abruptly wishing I had left it all alone, I was left with a single question: *What do I do now?* I fell into uneasy asleep then, my dreams a mishmash of this and that.

✳ ✳ ✳

A SHRILL RINGING JANGLED MY ears. Groggily opening one eye, I saw that my bedside clock read 5:10 a.m. I moaned and was just about to roll over when the ringing started again. This time, I realized it wasn't my alarm. It was my building's intercom. Groaning, I hauled myself out of bed, padded sleepily to the panel, and picked up the receiver.

"Hello," I said, my voice hoarse with sleep.

"Courier," the crisp voice announced.

"What?" I choked out, what he was saying failing to fully register in my brain.

"Courier. Picking up a package."

Even half-asleep, I know better than to absently buzz a random person into the building. "I don't have a package. You have the wrong address."

I was ready to hang up when the voice asked, "Are you Della Sanders?"

"Yes." I was now wide awake.

"We received a message for a pickup. All packaging and courier costs prepaid."

"I have no package," I stated, certain this was some type of hoax.

"I was told to mention that the message is from Buddy. That you'd understand." The voice stopped speaking and waited as I processed this.

Buddy?

"Give me a minute," I said, already reaching for my cell.

Clicking on the phone, I saw a final text from Buddy. "Courier arriving your place very early a.m. All costs prepaid. Haven't heard from you, so assuming all went well."

I sighed. Was I surprised? Maybe not.

"I'll be right down," I said to the voice. Pulling on sweats and stuffing the box into a plastic bag, I took the elevator down to the lobby. The indifferent courier took the wrapped metal chest and jammed it tightly inside a reinforced box before sealing it. As he handed me a receipt, I took special note of his name and employee number. Just in case.

Then I went upstairs and back to bed. Unfortunately, staring wide-eyed at the ceiling only brought up more questions. Finally, I got up and made coffee, checking my cell frequently throughout the day. Nothing.

The following morning, I sent a text. Short and simple. "Did the box arrive?" I pressed send. Immediately, a return message pinged. "Caller unknown."

I sighed, profoundly defeated.

Buddy was gone, and I suspected that I would never hear from him again.

He'd used my enduring loyalty one final time for his own personal gains. Do I *like* to think that? No. But I have come to terms with it.

For me, he will always be a real-life action hero who championed the rescue of a scared little girl with no one to turn to.

That's the Buddy I *choose* to remember.

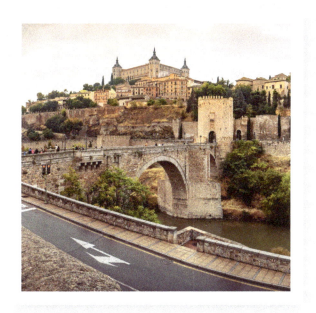

Holy Toledo

S UNBEAMS RICOCHETED THROUGH THE REVOLVING doors of
Madrid's Durham Hotel, reflecting a rainbow confection on a
giant crystal chandelier.

It's a sign. A good one, I stressed inwardly, needing desperately to
believe that.

Walking through the doors and entering the lobby, the reception
desk of the hotel loomed dauntingly before me.

"May I be of assistance, madam?" The man's voice resonated of
English high tea served in fine china cups.

"Um…" I started, frantically probing the depths of my purse for wallet and passport.

"Madam?" the voice repeated gently. I blinked, turning my gaze to a calm face adorned with a clipped moustache and elegant goatee. The dark eyes studying me expressed concern.

"Um…yes…uh…" I began again, forcing myself to take a deep breath and carry on. "Sorry. Yes, please…Um…I don't have a reservation," I finally blurted. Seeing the clerk open his mouth to respond, I added hastily, "but the taxi driver assured me—yes, *assured* me—that there would be no problem with that, even though it's June and tourist season, and…" I stopped long enough to take a breath, then added, "Five nights. That's all I need. I already tried three other hotels." I ended this babbling rant with a solitary plea, my eyes suddenly filling with tears. "Please."

Not knowing what else to say, I abruptly stopped talking. The restless shuffling of the queue that was forming behind me increased.

"One moment please, madam," he stated, his gaze sweeping past me. Taking a couple of steps backwards, he opened a barely discernible doorway. After a few words were spoken that I couldn't quite make out, a young woman stepped back through. Slipping effortlessly behind a neighbouring computer screen, she beckoned the next guests in line forward.

"Names, please," she requested as a young couple filled the space before her, and as their mumbled responses drifted across to me, the original clerk retook his spot directly in front of me. His quiet assessment of me was met with a serene, studying stare. I could only guess what was going through his mind. Or perhaps not.

Until yesterday, I'd been a reasonably self-assured woman in her middling fifties, wearing a navy suit and a white shirt. Twenty-four hours later, I was still sporting the same outfit, but no doubt was projecting a different image. My face felt covered in sticky residue like after a day at the beach. My luggage was a simple purple-sequined

backpack, emblazoned with the words "Go Girl, Go!" in irides-
cent pink.

The clerk's solitary glance seemed to take all of this in, but the
final result of this assessment was kept carefully concealed behind an
implacable facade.

With a small, crooked smile, he said, "One moment again please,
madam." Then he turned his face to the screen before him. Rapid
fingertips clattered a succession of keystrokes. A moment later, his
unruffled features and regard slipped back to me, offering a barely
perceptible nod.

"I think we have just the room for you," he announced simply.

I hadn't realized I was holding my breath until I exhaled. Beyond
elation, I couldn't stop smiling. *Everything is going to be okay,* I reasoned idiotically. *I have a room!*

"Thank you! That's wonderful!" I gushed. "Thank you *so* much!"

His smile in response was faint but seemed genuine. "Your passport and credit card please, madam."

Almost giddy with relief, I located both, and handed them over
joyfully, a rush of adrenaline pushing aside my exasperations and
fatigue. Everything was going to be okay. I just knew it.

Suddenly remembering the good manners my mother had spent a
lifetime drilling into her children, I checked his name tag. *Alexander.*
If there was a surname, I missed it as he handed me a small envelope
with a key card tucked safely inside.

"Thank you, Alexander," I gushed, openly ecstatic. I glanced at
the envelope. Room 617. *My new lucky number,* I thought inanely.
"You're a life saver. Truly."

His slight smile now seemed warm and inviting. "We hope you
enjoy your stay with us, Mrs. Starman. Currently, we have you registered with us for five nights. If something should change within that
time frame, please don't hesitate to let us know."

I knew what he was telling me: I was lucky to have a room. For
five nights only.

Leaning forward in an effort to keep my comments more confidential, I said in a rush, "Thank you again, Alexander. You have no idea what this means to me. Thank you so very much!"

Again, he nodded, his smile widening to show off his straight white teeth. Lifting his hand, Alexander signaled a porter. I was about to shrug off the assistance before remembering that porters, too, had to earn a livelihood.

Graciously, I relinquished the sparkling bag to the perplexed and earnest face of a young teen. Looking at first a bit bewildered, he quickly recovered. "This way, madam, if you please."

I remembered to check his nametag, learning that his name was Nicolas, and working to commit it to memory as I followed him to my room, offering him a tip once he'd placed my bag down.

Twenty euros. That's all it had taken to bring the hugest smile to Nicolas's face, making me wonder how generous it had been as I pressed the door quietly closed behind him.

"So, how much did I really just pay out?" I mumbled as I slid the security latch into place. "Probably quite a bit," I continued aloud. "Not that it matters. Oh, and by the way, have you heard they've started putting away old ladies who start talking to themselves?" I chuckled at this, and then answered my own question with a tired smirk. "Only if they catch them."

I finally had a room, and right now, that took precedence over anything else. Sinking into the opulent desk chair, upholstered in rich damask, I pushed off my shoes and looked down. My ankles were swollen. *What do you expect when you were at thirty thousand feet for ten hours?* Wriggling my toes, I studied my surroundings.

What the room lacked in size, it made up for in accoutrements. Matching sculptured bedspreads on twin beds sported an impressive array of green- and taupe-hued cushions. Two vibrant floral sketches hung on the wall above the bed, ensconced in bronze frames. The flowing lines of dark, classic furniture added a certain gravity to the room's carved desk and neighbouring armoire. No doubt, the latter would be cleverly concealing a television behind its closed front panels—one I firmly vowed not to ever use.

I'm escaping, I reminded myself. I didn't want televised reality clouding my focus. Standing up, I strolled to the window, pushing the heavy drapes aside. Through the gauzy inner lining, the room's view of the outside world was hardly worth mentioning. Just an alleyway, plus the rooftop of the adjacent building. Turning away, I walked to the bathroom. A click of the switch bathed the small white room in light. It looked bright and clean, with a huge mirror completing the setup.

"Perfect," I said sarcastically. "Just what I need: a reminder of how I look." I scowled at my reflection for a moment before my face split into a huge grin.

"I have a room!" I crowed triumphantly.

After a moment, I sobered somewhat, looking at my doppelgänger in the mirror. "So, what's the next part of your plan, genius?" The reflection stayed frustratingly silent.

My cell pinged then. Once. Twice. Three times. Sighing, I knew it was time to talk to the kids. This wasn't going to be an easy conversation. *Oh well. At least it won't be boring.*

I texted them: "Let's do a group video."

I worked to gather my scattered thoughts as the call began a few minutes later, and three distraught faces lit up before me, belonging to my daughters, Carmen and Cybil, and my daughter-in-law, Judith. My absentee son, Wyatt, always manages to avoid unpleasant business, like video calls. That was one trait, at least, that he'd picked up from me. Admittedly, not my best attribute.

Judith spoke first. "Theresa, where in God's green earth are you?! We've been trying to reach you since you texted that you were going away. It's been hours now! We were worried sick!"

I hadn't meant to worry them. A rush of guilt washed over me.

"I'm okay," I began, feeling my way forward in terms of what I was actually going to say. "I've just…Well, I've had a tough year, as you know, what with the problems between dad and I…"

Oh, God…I really didn't want to go there. It was too raw.

I pressed on. "You all know that it's been absolutely horrible at work for a long time now, and I've been trying to sort it out, but nothing changes. Yesterday, I'd just finally had enough and told them that I was taking some personal time."

Wow! Was that really only yesterday?

A rising babble of responding voices interrupted my thoughts, heavy with concern, which was hard to face. *Well, at least they don't seem angry.*

Staring into the small screen, I spoke back up. "I didn't mean to worry anyone. I'm *really* sorry," I stressed as another wave of guilt assaulted me. Taking a deep breath, I finally got to the point. "I'm in Madrid."

"Madrid?" Cybil blurted. "As in *Spain?*"

"Yeah, like that," I admitted, laughing hesitantly.

"Mom, seriously? That's on the other side of the planet!" Carmen added, her tone plainly troubled.

"Yeah, well…" My voice was trembling, as tears filled my eyes. "Your dad and I separating…Well, I'm not handling that too well, and then the work stuff kind of pushed me over the edge. I told my supervisor—"

Wait, I thought suddenly, snapping my mouth shut and stopping myself mid babble. "Listen, you have all heard me whining about all that a million times. I'm sure you're probably tired of it too, so there's no point rehashing it now. What matters is that I've taken some personal time. And as soon as I left work, I called a travel agency and asked if there was any kind of sell-off seat sale at the moment, or at least something that was leaving today—well, yesterday now, I suppose. I told the woman who'd answered that I didn't care where it was going. As long as it was somewhere else.

"Anyway," I continued, "she mentioned a few available destinations, and Madrid struck a chord, so I booked the ticket. I stopped at home just long enough to pick up my passport and few essentials." I didn't bother clarifying that the only thing I'd grabbed besides the passport was my toothbrush and makeup bag. I'd actually ended up buying the backpack at the airport, just to have some kind of luggage with me.

Feeling suddenly self-conscious, I shook my head slightly. "It sounds so crazy now, saying it all out loud," I admitted, then tried to laugh it off. "Yep. Your loony mom is having her mid-life crisis a little late!"

I breathed a bit easier when I was finally rewarded with smiles from all three of them.

"So, what happens now?" Judith asked in a serious tone a moment later.

"Oh, Judith," I said with a huge sigh. "If I knew that, I might have actually thought things through before ending up in a random hotel room in Spain. I honestly don't know. I have five days before flying back, so I guess I'll mainly be doing a lot of thinking. Figuring stuff out."

"What about Dad?" Carmen asked a bit awkwardly. "When we couldn't find you, we checked with him—just in case you were there. Obviously, you weren't, but he's worried now. What should we tell him?"

I was touched by Daryl's concern. "Carmen, honey, it's fine. Just tell your dad what I've just told you." Despite my casual words, I still felt kind of uncomfortable talking about their father, so I abruptly changed the subject. "Listen, how about we connect in a couple of days and chat again. In the meantime, I'll text to keep you all posted, okay?"

Everyone agreed, and after a few minutes of exchanging pleasantries, we disconnected. Then exhaustion set in. Lying on the bed,

I closed my eyes, realizing that I should really be adjusting my sleep pattern to the local time zone. Instead, I fell fast asleep.

∗ ∗ ∗

A COUPLE OF DAYS LATER, as I crossed the hotel lobby, I noticed a quiet moment at the reception desk. Taking advantage of the fact that Alexander was alone, I walked over to him.

"I hope I'm not interrupting?"

He looked up and smiled. "Not at all, Mrs. Starman," he answered pleasantly. "What can I assist you with?"

"Nothing at all, really. I just wanted to thank you for the information on local shopping. I've managed to purchase a few things," I said, lifting my shopping bags.

"Very glad to hear that. If there's anything else you require, please don't hesitate to let me know."

"Thanks. I will."

Just as I turned away, he spoke again. "Mrs. Starman, I wonder if you would be interested in seeing some sights? There is a tour-bus excursion this morning. Just for the day. I could give you some details if you think that's something you would like to do."

"Really? Where?" I asked. Not used to having time on my hands, I was feeling somewhat out of sorts.

Consulting his computer screen briefly, he said, "The bus leaves at eleven this morning for Toledo. Approximately an hour's drive. A walking tour through the city with a local guide is included in the cost. There is still space available. If you like, I can reserve you a seat."

"I would still have my room when I get back?" I asked, suddenly panicked, hoping this wasn't just a soft method of maneuvering me out of the hotel.

"Absolutely, Mrs. Starman," he said reassuringly. "It is a day trip only," he repeated gently.

"Sounds lovely," I replied, suddenly excited by the prospect. "Toledo, you said?"

"Yes, that's correct. If I may say, I highly recommend it. You won't be disappointed." He stopped then, awaiting my confirmation.

Hmm…Toledo. I had never heard of it but made an instant decision. "Yes, thank you. I think I'd like to go."

"I will include you then."

"Thank you, Alexander," I said happily, glad to have a scheduled activity. "I'll just drop these bags in my room and be back shortly."

✳ ✳ ✳

THE LUXURY BUS CAME COMPLETE with a cooler of cold drinks and snacks, plus Manny, our congenial guide. Tour-group headphones made it easy for us to listen to his loquacious explanations of the sights along the way.

Nearly an hour later, the bus pulled over at a small roadside rest stop. I looked around. Was there a problem?

"There is nothing wrong, I assure you," Manny said soothingly, noting a few concerned faces. "I simply wanted to prepare you for a spectacular view just beyond the next curve, where we will be stopping for photos." With a big smile, he motioned to the driver, who pulled back onto the road.

When we turned the corner in question, what met our eyes was singularly jaw-dropping. A collective gasp rang throughout the bus. If there was a moment in time worth freezing into a single frame, this was it.

Someone quietly breathed out the words "Oh, my God!"

Exactly.

Beyond the width of a deep river gorge, and atop the opposing cliff, Toledo stretched its magnificence over a craggy landscape. A medieval metropolis enmeshed in a dazzling compilation of cathedral spires, minarets, fortress towers, and bastion turrets.

Mystical. Magical. Humbling.

Exiting the bus with the others and completely spellbound, I could only stare, a calm serenity sweeping over me. The suffocating insecurity and overwhelming panic that had been hounding me dimmed in the glory I was seeing in the distance. I couldn't explain it, but a sudden courage and confidence settled inside me then.

There was one person—and only one—with whom I would have given anything to be sharing this moment: Daryl. He would understand. He would see what I was seeing: History. Romance.

Pulling out my mobile, I tried not to overthink or change my mind. Pressing Daryl's number, I waited for him to pick up.

"Hi, Theresa," he said, having recognized my number. "Surprised to hear from you. The kids said you're in Spain. Everything okay?"

His voice told me he still cared, and since that was what I wanted to believe anyway, I believed it.

"I love you," I said simply, ignoring his question. "Is it too late for us? Please…Please, I need to hear that there's still a chance."

I waited, the seconds seeming to go on forever as my heart raced.

"Are you sure, Tee?" he asked. "You were so sure—"

"That's because I'm an idiot," I muttered inanely, suddenly feeling foolish and wishing desperately that he was with me now. "I'm in Toledo," I added, as if that would somehow mean something to him.

"Toledo?" His tone of voice echoed with the same uncertainty as mine had when I'd first heard the name.

"Yeah," I said, searching for what else to add.

After a moment, he said simply, "Come home, Tee. Okay? Just come home, and we'll talk. Work things out. I promise that I'll listen, but you'll have to do the same. Are you ready for that?"

It was then that I started crying and couldn't stop. I didn't even care who was watching. I was just so happy. "I will! I promise!" I finally blubbered. "I'm home day after tomorrow. I'll call when I get there. Then we'll talk. Okay?"

"I'll do you one better. Text me your flight details. I'll pick you up at the airport. Just come home." His tone seemed hopeful and sounded like second chances.

Alexander had been right. Toledo hadn't been a disappointment at all. Instead, it had shown me a way home that I'd never thought existed. Lifting my eyes skyward, I savoured the sun's warmth on my cheeks for a long moment as I breathed out a silent thank you to the universe.

A Dirty Business

Is this all somebody's idea of a joke? Duncan pondered silently. *And if so, then whose?*

Some five years earlier, his brainchild, JD Investigations, had been coddled into existence, a team combining his own techy skills, Jeff's legal training, and the money of MacGaskell Lewis (aka Muggy). To date, it had always been a winning combination. In all honesty though, without the funding infusion from Lewis Enterprises, the idea would never have seen daylight except through the grimy windows of the pub where it had been born.

Frustration crowded Duncan's thoughts. Standing up, he crossed the room and plunked a thin blue folder, labelled "Eleanor Buckman," on Jeff's desk.

"So, you're done," Jeff said, looking up. He leaned back in his chair, grinning at his partner.

"In more ways than one," growled Duncan, scowling as he plopped himself into the visitor chair opposite him. It protested audibly at the sudden weight. "I blame that little twerp, Muggy," he lamented.

A frown replaced Jeff's grin. "Muggy? I thought this was a simple background search?"

"No. And don't get me started on Muggy. If it wasn't for him, I never would have met you or found myself in this stupid detection business. Which means I wouldn't be sitting here right now trying to figure out what the *hell's* going on!" Tipping back, Duncan ran his fingers through his thinning hair in frustration.

"Okay, okay," Jeff said impatiently. "Enough. What's going on?"

"I'd tell you if I knew!"

Jeff sighed heavily, and then—trying to ease the tension with a very old memory—he asked, "What were the names of those goons who were attacking Muggy that day anyway? When we were kids, I mean."

"Who knows?" Duncan shrugged, knowing what his friend was doing but getting sidetracked anyway. "Goon One and Goon Two. Probably serving time as we speak. One thing I do know for sure though." For the first time, the barest hint of a smile appeared. "My mom was really ticked off about my tooth!"

Jeff couldn't help but laugh just thinking about Muggy, and Duncan chuckled reluctantly as well as he remembered the day in question.

Muggy had been running as fast as his short legs could manage, trying to get away from his attackers, but he'd forgotten all about the surrounding schoolyard fence and found himself properly cornered. Two against one. Other kids had started crowding close. No one had intervened, unwilling to risk becoming the next target, but everyone had been keen on witnessing the action, Jeff and Duncan included.

Years later, they had each accused the other of having been the one to issue a silent dare to rush the bullies, but either way, that was exactly what they'd done, charging in together. Though the element of surprise placed the odds of an implausible victory initially in their favour, the two seven-year-olds had quickly been outclassed by their opponents' size and weight advantage. However, their intervention had given Muggy the chance he'd needed to escape, and he'd taken it eagerly, sprinting for the safety of the school.

"It could have been worse," Jeff said. "Imagine if Muggy's little sister hadn't nabbed Coach Carson." He laughed again suddenly. "It's usually brothers rescuing their sisters, not the other way around. Too bad you and I don't have loyal sisters like Darcy! We were lucky to just end up with bloody noses and a few scrapes!"

"Hey! Don't you go forgetting about my chipped tooth," Duncan urged, his sullen mood momentarily slipping away. Then he gave Jeff a look, stood up, and picked the folder back up before plunking himself in his own desk chair. Opening it, he took a deep breath, preparing himself to share its contents with his partner. "Okay, here goes. Oh, and by the way, Jeff, I'll have a doozy of a question for you when I get to the end."

Settling in, Duncan scanned his notes and started sharing what he found there, elaborating as he went along: "Eleanor Buckman. Late thirties. Part-time receptionist for a local residential construction firm. Evenings and occasional weekends. Been there about three months. Gets paid in cash. No benefits or bonuses. Basically, a warm body to greet potential buyers before they're hustled off by salesmen. No driver's license. No passport. No credit or debit cards. She paid cash up front on a six-month apartment lease. She does have a chequing account at a local bank, but there's only enough in there to show her as a registered client. No investments or pension plan assets that I could find."

"No cell phone either," he continued, "just a landline. The only calls appear to be work related…schedule changes and the like. Hasn't got a personal computer or laptop. Doesn't even use public internet or access social-media sites. Pays cash for everything, including a piano!" He held up one hand, his eyes still fixed on the pages before him. "And before you ask, no, I'm not kidding! She must literally pull money out of her mattress every morning because I don't know where else she could be getting it. All that to say, I decided that I really needed to see this woman in person." He looked up and gave Jeff an assessing look.

"What?" Jeff asked, puzzled.

"Nothing," Duncan said, shaking his head and continuing. "Anyway, I went to the show-home location where she's working, thinking that I'd pretend to be interested in buying into the area." He snorted at his own thought. "As if I need to purchase another house, just to have the next woman who divorces me wrangle it away!"

"Need I remind you," Jeff patiently pointed out, "that you've sworn off women? Even dating them, let alone marrying one. Oh, by the way, Ginny has a cousin—"

Duncan's stern look silenced him mid-thought. Ignoring the potential relevance of this cousin, he brought the discussion back to business, this time without consulting the paperwork. Instead, his gaze was focusing distractedly out the window towards the parking lot. "In any case, I picked a Saturday to go see her because it seemed a good bet that all the salesmen would be busy, and I'd probably be left cooling my heels for a bit. That part went beautifully. Warmed a bench, along with a few others, for about twenty minutes, which gave me enough time to chat with Eleanor. She was friendly, but not too friendly, flashing smiles appropriately and laughing at my jokes."

That would be important, Jeff thought, smiling inwardly.

"In the end though, she couldn't wait to hustle me off to silver-tongued Lyle. I technically learned very little and actually came away with more questions than I'd arrived with." He stopped and gave Jeff another look.

"So?" Jeff asked, rolling his eyes a bit. "Get to the point already!"

Duncan stood up, walked over to his partner, and leaned down, resting his fists on the desktop. "Aren't you going to ask me what my 'doozy' of a question is?" he challenged with stinging sarcasm.

Stumped at Duncan's snarky attitude, Jeff opened his mouth to spit out exactly that question, but Duncan stopped him impatiently, waving it off. "Never mind. So—and it's a *big* 'so'—what I want to know is this: What was Muggy's *sister* doing, getting all dolled up and pretending to be this Eleanor what's-her-name person?! *That's* what *I* want to know!"

"*Darcy?!*" Jeff was stunned. "What?! You mean that Eleanor is *actually* Muggy's sister?" He was just about to ask another question when his cell phone buzzed. He looked down at the display, and then up again to meet Duncan's even gaze. "Muggy," he said simply, then swiped to answer.

"You're on speaker," Jeff declared, "and Dunc's with me."

"Great, great!" Muggy's voice filled the office. He sounded agitated.

Jeff frowned. "Mugg—"

"Listen," Muggy said, interrupting, "I need to see you both. Meet me at Twitchy's. It's about Eleanor." Then he hung up.

Duncan and Jeff shared puzzled looks.

* * *

THE GET-AWAY WAS A NEIGHBOURHOOD pub situated in an area that used to be right at the city limits. Now it was tucked inside a series of walk-ups, scattered high-rises, and the occasional strip malls. It had somehow survived all comers. Its owner was a grizzled ex-military man known to everyone simply as Twitchy. He had apparently originally purchased the property intending to refurbish the old establishment. Instead, he'd adopted the pub's eclectic clientele, who'd convinced him to leave well enough alone. "*If it ain't broke, don't fix it.*"

As Jeff and Duncan entered the dimly lit interior, they spotted Twitchy, who gestured at them, indicating that they should head towards the small room at the back. Jeff nodded, threading through tables already crowded for mid-afternoon, smiling hello to several familiar faces. They entered the door marked "Private" and closed it behind them. Muggy and Darcy were already there. Four frothy pints of ale in iced glasses graced the table.

Muggy looked tense, but then Muggy always looked tense. Many in the business world often misread that look as nervousness, rather than a carefully cultivated persona to confuse the competition and conceal a brilliant mind. It worked. Lewis Enterprises had their tentacles in countless interests, from baby products to technological innovations. Brother and sister sat side by side, Muggy, short and square, and Darcy, small and spare.

"Hello, *Eleanor,*" Duncan said.

"Hello, *Duncan,*" responded Darcy in kind. "Nice to see you again so soon," she finished smoothly.

"I can explain," began Muggy.

"You'd better," Duncan said, swiftly swilling a mouthful of the cold ale. Through the mock anger, an easy camaraderie cycled through the room, making it clear that these were old and trusted friends. Muggy lost his tenseness, or at least a portion of it. It was too long established to disappear completely.

"Duncan, you did a great job," said Muggy.

Duncan grunted. Compliments usually swayed him, but he wasn't about to succumb easily this time.

"I knew that if *you* couldn't break Darcy's cover," Muggy continued, "then she was safe."

"Cover?" Jeff added, speaking up as his gaze settled on each of them in turn. "What's that supposed to mean? What's going on?"

"I'll tell you everything," Muggy said, "but there's a favour I'm asking at the end of it, okay? Just thought I'd let you both know that up front."

Jeff and Duncan shared a look. Past experience had been a keen teacher. Muggy's "favours" were generally a little more complicated than that.

"Okay, 'fess up," pushed Duncan.

Muggy leaned forward, eyes alight. The businessman was at work. "You remember old man Ryan? Billy Ryan? The family farmed out past Range Road 79, way out in the sticks." He didn't wait for confirmation and just continued. "Well, when Darcy and I were kids, Mrs. Ryan—Rose, her name was—would sometimes babysit us at their place for a few days while our folks were away. They had two sons about our age, Garth and Rob. You remember them, right?" This time he waited and was rewarded with vague nods from Jeff and Duncan.

"Well, Rose Ryan passed on about ten years back, and Billy's in a nursing home. Pretty crippled up with arthritis, but I take him out for lunch from time to time." As cunning an entrepreneur as Muggy was, and as hard as he tried to hide it, no one had a kinder heart. "Well, Billy's been itching to see the old homestead. Both Garth and Ron moved away a couple years ago, and he's barely seen them or their families since. He seems to have accepted that but would like to see the old farm and what the new owners have done with it. I've managed to put him off, thinking maybe I should have a quick look to make sure it's presentable enough for him. I didn't want him to see it if it's been allowed to go to seed. I finally decided one day to just drive out and get it done."

He stopped then, a strange look coming over his face. "You know how sometimes you think you've seen and heard it all and that no one can surprise you anymore? And then, wham, something hits you in the head and knocks you sideways?" He paused. He definitely had Jeff and Duncan's complete attention. Darcy was also fully engaged, but it was evident that nothing Muggy was going to say would be a surprise to her.

Staring into the distance as if in a trance, his voice grew deathly quiet. He spoke as if still in disbelief. "The Ryans had about five thousand acres. I still remember the roar of the combines, the smell of hay and grain, and dust flying behind us." He sounded almost reverent. Darcy touched the back of his hand lightly.

"It's gone," Muggy whispered, tears filming his eyes.

"Gone?" Jeff echoed. "What's gone?"

"Everything!" His eyes and voice hardened. "Just what I said. The first thing I noticed was the ten-foot-high barbed-wire fence that stretched as far as I could see. I drove around as much of it as I could, where it had road access. The farmhouse and all the buildings were gone. There's not a tree or a shrub or even a blade of grass. You see, there couldn't possibly be... *There's no soil,*" he finished darkly. "No dirt. Just rocks and clay. It's been totally stripped. All of it!"

"No dirt?" repeated Duncan, frowning. He couldn't comprehend what he was hearing.

"It gets more interesting," continued Muggy, his agitation mounting. "I got stopped by a patrol vehicle. I'm serious. A couple of thug-types asking what I was doing out there. I just said I was lost and acted really happy to see them. It was all so weird. Felt like I was in some sci-fi movie. When I got home, I sat down and had a stiff drink. Or maybe it was two. I thought of a lot of things, like going back to take photos or even sending out a drone to do that. I don't think I slept all night."

Darcy looked at Duncan. "Muggy called me in the morning. Damn early, as I remember." She gave him a not so gentle look. "I think I nearly ripped his head off, but it felt important, so I hustled myself over to his place. We talked for hours. Figured out we needed more information and didn't want to draw attention to ourselves. Between the two of us, we came up with 'Eleanor.' I needed access to a computer and internet. The construction-company reception position seemed perfect. It's a piece of cake researching land titles and such when it looks legit."

"But I needed to make sure she was safe," stressed Muggy. "We both figured that if you couldn't find a loose end in her cover, Duncan, no one else would figure out who she really was or what she was doing."

Darcy smiled crookedly at Duncan. "You really gave me a start when you turned up. I just prayed you wouldn't give me away."

Duncan shook his head, any remnants of anger long since dissipated. "I nearly did, especially after all the work I'd done. But then I figured something was in the works, so I just zipped it. I actually thought Jeff was having me on in some way, but he gave me the same stupid look when I tried putting it to him as he's giving right now."

Smiling wryly, it was Jeff's turn to shake his head.

Darcy grew serious. "I checked land sales and did some searches. So far, there are seven other farms stripped down the same as Mr. Ryan's. All of them are fairly isolated properties and distanced enough from one another so as not to raise any red flags or eyebrows from nosy neighbours."

"So," Jeff said, summarizing, "someone's stealing dirt?"

"Exactly," Muggy nodded.

"But why?" chorused Jeff and Duncan.

"Well," Muggy said, putting his thoughts together slowly, "this could be a long shot, but I've been keeping an eye on agricultural journals. Not to name names, but say there are some countries who've been reporting huge agricultural successes and using climate change as their focal point for these miracles. These places are better situated in the world for sunshine. Manipulating rainfall techniques is an added bonus. The only thing really lacking is rich soil…good old Mother Earth, in effect. They're not drawing attention to methods, just results, with crops that haven't been produced there in decades or even centuries. All this is done very low-key. One wouldn't actually know about it if you weren't specifically looking."

"That just sounds crazy, Muggy!" Duncan said, frowning.

"Think about it," Muggy said earnestly. "If a country can make itself agriculturally self-sufficient, then it doesn't have to rely on other countries' trade practices. Eventually, if there's enough massive soil pillaging, whole countries could be ruined. Darcy and I think there's a lot more than just the eight we've found so far just from a relatively small land search. What about the rest of the country?"

"You're talking like this is some kind of conspiracy!" Duncan said, shaking his head. "That's nuts!"

"No, it's not," stressed Muggy. "Think of all the things that people have done for those two five-letter words: money and power."

Jeff didn't want to hear any more. "So, what's the favour?" His eyes never left Muggy's face.

Muggy inhaled deeply and exhaled slowly. "I want the two of you to investigate this and find how deep it goes. If I'm right, this crosses all political borders and boundaries from local right up to federal. A lot of palms have been greased to make this happen. I have to be honest here," and he gave them each a long look, "I can't tell you all this without adding that it could be dangerous. I don't want you to underestimate that factor."

Duncan took a last swallow of his ale while Jeff sat in contemplation. "Okay, Muggy," Jeff said finally. "What's all this got to do with you?"

Muggy looked pensively at his sister. "Darcy and I were born with the proverbial silver spoons, but it didn't come for free. We've always believed in giving back. Because of Lewis Enterprises, I—or rather, we—need to steer clear, for the time being, at least. All investigation has to be done totally above board and not be interpreted as us dipping our oar in and muddying the situation for our own benefit. Once all completed data is independently analyzed and verified, we'll step back in. Expose it. Just not sure how yet."

Jeff and Duncan sat quietly for a moment, each in their own thoughts, as Duncan twirled his empty glass.

Suddenly, a muted cheer arose from the pub crowd on the other side of the door. A warm breath of reality. It seemed to settle something for Duncan. He turned to Jeff and said matter-of-factly, "I did dare you, actually. I thought I could take Goon One by myself, but didn't know if I could do the same with Goon Two." He shrugged apologetically.

Muggy and Darcy shared glances that seemed to say, *"That old story again."*

A slow smile stretched across Jeff's face, before he sobered and shook his head. "You really are a SOB, aren't you?"

"We have an even bigger question," Duncan said, thoughtfully.

Jeff raised his eyebrows. *"Oh, yes?"*

"How many beers will it take to seal this deal?"

"Twitchy!" they all called in unison, holding their empty glasses aloft.

* * *

A FEW WEEKS INTO FULL-TILT research, Duncan and Jeff each received an urgent text: "Lewis Enterprises. 20 minutes."

Duncan and Jeff shared astonished looks. Both had been expecting another get-together to share info. This was something else entirely. The location parlayed the message that this was something official. Dire, even.

Muggy was giving them a veiled heads-up.

On their arrival at the office, there was an unexpected guest there, in addition to Muggy and Darcy. It was Twitchy. This seemed odd, but neither Jeff nor Duncan commented. As the owner of the Get-Away, Twitchy was always in the background and even occasionally joined the foursome during their monthly pub nights there. Seemed a great guy but always a bit stand-offish. More Muggy's friend, really. All decked out in a suit and tie, he was barely recognizable now as a barkeeper.

Jeff and Duncan had agreed beforehand to play a wait-and-see game in terms of what kind of a hand was being dealt. Twitchy's inclusion meant that endeavours had shifted into unknown parameters. There was a definite edge to the atmosphere, and his presence was obviously part of that equation.

In an all-business tone, Muggy got started. "I know you're both wondering why Twitchy is here. Actually, I should maybe use Twitchy's real name and—"

"Not necessary," said Twitchy brusquely. "I assure you." The hint of a smile on his lips didn't quite reach his eyes. "Let's just stick with Twitchy, okay?" Despite the questioning "okay," this statement sounded more like a command than any sort of opening for discussion.

The room stayed silent.

"Okay, Twitchy," said Muggy, his voice tight. "I'm going to let you do most of the talking here to give the official version of the situation to date. Afterwards, we can have an open-question session, assuming that there are any questions." His meaning was evident. There would be.

Duncan shifted in his seat, all concentration. Jeff looked a bit more puzzled than anything.

Twitchy stepped smoothly into his new role while simultaneously shedding that of a barman. "I'm just going to launch right in. You all know I'm ex-military. Been out of that for a number of years, but I still have affiliations with former crew mates who have moved up into certain areas of government."

Duncan and Jeff shared a look at the word "government," but Twitchy wasn't done. "I know where you guys currently are within the investigation and research on—"

"Dirty Business," interrupted Jeff. "That's the name we gave this project. Kind of seemed appropriate."

Twitchy smiled humourlessly. "Okay, well, Dirty Business has proven to be a bit of a big deal. I understand that you've uncovered upwards of thirty properties across the country so far that have had the same thing happen to them as what Muggy saw." He paused meaningfully and gave a hard look to Jeff and Duncan. "But as of right now, any further research into this is officially terminated. No more. Done. Got it?"

"What?!" Duncan snapped, jumping to his feet. "What's this about?"

Muggy spoke up now, his voice heavy with finality. "It's done, Duncan."

Duncan wasn't finished though and confronted Twitchy. "Okay, what the hell is really going on? Our country is being pillaged, and you're treating the whole situation as if it's nothing! Is anything being done to *fix* the damage? Shutting something down like this sounds exactly like a big, fat, government-type no. What's with that?"

"Okay, Muggs," Jeff said. "What gives here? Seriously."

Muggy gave Twitchy a severe look. "They're right. That's a copout," he said harshly. "Frankly, I think it's only fair that they get to hear the rest, or at least more than just that."

Twitchy said nothing.

With a grunt of frustration, Muggy turned his back on the man and took matters into his own hands. "Okay, here goes. I basically got my hands slapped on this thing. Hard. But I will tell you that the whole situation got leaked somehow to government insiders who weren't included in the original knowledge base. Ruffled some high mucky-mucks pretty good. Right now, it's even on the radar of a very outspoken journalist. One who's always looking to dig up some dirt. No pun intended. He has his own investigation going and—"

"That guy's progress has been officially hobbled," Twitchy said firmly. "It's done, guys. Accept it."

"So, that's it?!" Duncan was furious. "We're right on the cusp of proving how widespread this is, and now you're saying that we can't? So, do we get to tell our side of the story? About what's really happening?" Duncan looked straight at Muggy.

Muggy sighed defeatedly, giving him a resigned look. "No."

"No?" Jeff echoed incredulously, finally finding his voice. "So, we're just supposed to let it lie?" He shook his head. "I don't accept that. The story should be leaked to everyone so we can air things out about what the hell has been going on!" He looked to Duncan for confirmation.

"Absolutely not," Twitchy said, his tone firm and threatening. "As it is, it took some doing just to keep everyone in this room from being charged with some kind of crime. This is serious stuff."

"Someone else commits the deed, and *we're* going to be charged!" Duncan roared "What kind of BS is that? What the hell is happening here?" He looked around the room for support. Darcy started to say something, but Muggy touched her arm. She looked at him in dismay.

Twitchy sneered. "Duncan, Jeff, you guys think you can beat this somehow, but this is coming down from the highest government echelons. There is *nothing* that can be done. And they want everything you've discovered. All your information. Laptops. The works. You guys get it now? This isn't something that can somehow be negotiated. It's either this or charges will be laid. You can't win either way."

Duncan's jaw clenched as he shared a look with Jeff. "And when *exactly* are they showing up to take everything?"

"Couple of hours," Twitchy answered. "I'm only letting you guys in on it because Muggy said that he would if I didn't. Figured you should hear from some kind of an official source instead."

"Okay," said Duncan, suddenly very quiet and totally submissive. "Sure, no problem. If that's the way it has to be, that's the way it's going to be." His eyes narrowed slightly as he gave Jeff a pointed look.

A moment later, Jeff shrugged. "Yeah. No problem. We'll get everything ready."

With that, the pair looked at Muggy and Darcy.

"You guys understand, right?" Darcy said then, not quite believing their sudden acquiescence. "Everything goes to the authorities. *Everything.*" Her voice had a nearly hysterical edge to it.

"No problem," Duncan and Jeff chorused.

Turning to Duncan, Jeff said quietly, "Well, I guess we'd better get over to the office and get it all gathered together before the goons show up."

"Absolutely," agreed Duncan. "See you guys later."

Without another word, he and Jeff left the room.

Twitchy looked completely bewildered. "I don't get what just happened. Everything's okay then, right?" He looked to Muggy and Darcy for reassurance. "They're going to hand everything over?"

"That's what they said, so I can only assume that's what's going to happen," Muggy confirmed laconically.

While not fully understanding, Darcy nonetheless followed her brother's lead, adding, "It's all done, Twitchy. You can relax. Duncan and Jeff are no fools. They know when they're beaten."

"Okay," Twitchy said, looking at one and then the other. "That's really all I wanted to make sure of. I'll let my contacts know. They'll take care of the rest."

"Thanks, Twitchy. Much appreciated," said Muggy, his face inscrutable.

Twitchy nodded. Something was amiss, but he couldn't put his finger on what it was. That feeling followed him as he left the room.

The door closed behind him. For a minute, Muggy and Darcy said nothing, each busy with their own thoughts.

Finally, Muggy spoke up. "Remember all those years back when you ran to get Coach Carson while Jeff and Duncan were jumping those goons?"

"Kind of. What's that got to do with anything?" Darcy was feeling even more befuddled than Twitchy.

"Well, Duncan and Jeff got it all figured out that there's some serious goon activity going on right now. I'm thinking they're probably working on a plan to hand everything over while still making sure that the history of it all doesn't go down the drain. Like it did with the Avro Arrow. If I know those guys, Duncan especially, they're not going to take this lying down. In the meantime, there are two things that I've got to do."

"And they are?" asked Darcy, slowing cluing in.

"Got to get a trip for Billy Ryan organized. Maybe set up a couple of weeks in Hawaii for him and a few of his cronies." He paused, sadness creeping into his voice. "Convince him to look forward and not back."

"You said two things. What's the second?"

Muggy sighed. "Need to find a new pub. Just saw something I didn't much like."

Darcy nodded; then her brow furrowed. "Hey, you mentioned something about the Avro Arrow? What the heck is that?"

"Forgotten history, little sister," he smiled benevolently. "Make yourself comfortable, and I'll fill you in."

Uncle Brian

LYING ON A TROLLEY BENEATH an old Chevy, Brian heard a vehicle drive up and stop, followed by a slamming door and running feet.

"We've got company, Rufus," he muttered to a big grey cat dozing in the corner.

The car drove away, even as the shop's door opened.

"Hi, Uncle Bri," the voice said.

Stacey.

Brian was actually a little surprised. She was to have been here five days ago and supposedly every day since. Stacey was the one who had first approached Louise, telling her that she wanted to earn some money and asking her aunt for ideas.

Yeah, right, Brian had thought at the time. To be fair, a portion of Stacey's statement had rung true. She did want money, but earning it was something else entirely.

Brian rolled reluctantly out from beneath the car. Staring up at his niece, he was initially taken aback by her attire. Some kind of halter-top and mini-shorts combo. Well, whatever. Since she was here to clean the house before Louise arrived back from her trip down east, he didn't much care what she wore. His surprise stemmed mostly from the fact that his brother-in-law, Lloyd, had even allowed her out of the house dressed like that. Again, whatever.

"Hey, Stace, great to see you," he said cheerfully. Sitting up, he grabbed a rag and slowly wiped grease from his fingers. Frowning, he wondered fleetingly why she wasn't in the house doing the job Louise had hired her for. Feeling at a bit of a disadvantage on the floor, he stood up.

"So, how's everything going?" he continued, thinking he should be saying something. "Enjoying spring break?"

"Uh...all's good, Uncle Bri." She paused, suddenly looking slightly uncomfortable.

Of course, Brian thought, *sixteen-year-old girls. Who really knows them, eh?* Anyway, he didn't have time for chit-chat. He was just about to squat back down to the roller board when she said, "I was thinking I might pop into town to pick up some cleaning supplies. Could I maybe get a few bucks from you and borrow your car?"

"Sure," answered Brian easily. "There's some loose change and bills in the basket on the kitchen cupboard. The keys to my car are hanging on the hook in the porch. Heck, Stace," he added with a laugh. "Why am I telling you? You know where to find everything."

"Uh, okay, sure. Thanks, Uncle Bri," she said brightly. With that, she was gone.

Brian rolled back under the car and did a slow count to twenty before he heard the door opening, and she re-entered the garage.

"U-Uncle Brian..." she began, haltingly.

"Yeah?" he replied but didn't roll out from under the car this time. He already had a sense of what she was going to say.

"Well, there's only about ten bucks in that basket, plus your car is kind of weird."

"Weird?" replied Brian in feigned innocence. "What do you mean, weird?" Again, he waited.

"Well, I can't get it to start."

This time, he rolled out and stood up. "Hmph. That's strange. Used it last night, and it worked just fine. I know you got your driver's license last month. Maybe I should have asked you first, but you do know how to drive a manual now, right?"

"Manual?" Her tone rang with total confusion.

"Yeah, you know. A stick? Five-speed?"

Her look stayed blank. Finally, she just shrugged.

"The Subaru's a manual transmission, Stacey," Brian explained patiently. "I thought maybe, when you took your lessons, you'd learned on a manual." That was a lie. He'd known, even while in the midst of his explanation, that there was no way Stacey would ever have done more than what was deemed absolutely necessary. He'd just wanted to hear what she had to say.

Brian had already heard a week's worth of excuses from both Lloyd and Yvonne for why their daughter hadn't shown up for even one day of her school spring break to actually *do* the house-cleaning job offer she had gratefully accepted from Louise. His annoyance right now was just the perfect fuel for a well-oiled conversation.

"Uh, no. I learned on an automatic. Maybe I could just borrow Auntie Louise's car?" Her voice resonated with hopeful optimism.

Brian wiped a dirty hand across his mouth to still a threatening smile. "Sorry, kid. Would love to lend it to you, but it's got a flat.

Thanks for the reminder though. Need to fix that before she gets back tomorrow."

Stacey looked totally lost, but Brian wasn't having any of it. He'd had more than enough of Lloyd's kids always running rough shod over him. Well, mostly over Louise, really, but she couldn't seem to deal with it at all. Lloyd was the baby of her family and had been coddled forever. Now in his forties, he still managed to get everyone to dance to whatever tune he was playing. And he had easily passed that same trait on down to his kids.

Brian knew also that he would never win any kind of battle of wills here, but he wasn't going to go down easily. Not outwardly anyway. That was for sure.

"Listen, Stacey, I'm sure there's loads of cleaning stuff in the cupboard. Auntie L doesn't usually run out of that kind of thing. Just go in there, and do the best you can. You know where the vacuum and everything else is. How about I just leave you to get to it, okay?"

Stacey looked completely crestfallen, though Brian could almost hear her brain whirring through the information she'd just received. He waited. After a second or two of continued silence, he added nonchalantly, "Everything okay?" Then he stooped down, preparing once more to roll out of sight.

"You know what, Uncle Brian? You're right. I'll just go in and check what there is. If I have to, I might get my girlfriend, Rachel, to pick me up, and we can run into town."

"Whatever works for you, Stace," said Brian. "Just a reminder that your aunt's back home tomorrow. Early flight, I think."

"Right," she answered, already on autopilot. With that, she turned around, pulling her cell from her back pocket as she walked. Fingers busily texting, she strolled outside, not bothering to even shut the shop door behind her.

"Well, Rufus, what do you think the next move's going to be?" asked Brian pensively. Rufus didn't stir. "I'm thinking we can probably each take a guess and be right on both counts. No doubt she'll get away with her actions. She always does, but…" He paused meaningfully. "Well, if so, it'll definitely be without my help." With that, he rolled back out of sight, humming a tune to himself.

SOME MOMENTS LATER, WHILE BRIAN was engrossed in trying to unscrew a bolt that steadfastly refused to cooperate, he heard another vehicle arrive. A few footfalls on the gravel, followed by a car door opening and closing, and then the car driving away. He couldn't help but smile, knowing without checking that Stacey was gone. Brian rolled out just enough to be able to glance at the shop's clock. It was pushing one p.m. Instantly, he made a silent bet with himself that he wouldn't see her till at least four. Using historical behaviour as a marker, maybe not even then.

It was hunger pangs that finally convinced Brian to call it a day. He rolled out one final time from under the car's belly. Another look at the clock. Just past 3:30 and still no Stacey.

Suddenly, his cell rang from the work bench. He sauntered over and pressed the button to connect the call with one extended finger. "Hey, bro. You're on speaker. My hands are a bit greasy here. What can I do you for, Lloyd?"

"Listen, I've been calling Stacey's cell, and she isn't answering. I figured I might come and pick her up about four-thirty or five. Thought she might be finishing up by then."

Brian answered lazily, forcing a thoughtful tone into his voice. "Well, Lloyd, I honestly don't think she's back yet. She took a few bucks for cleaning supplies to get whatever it was that she needed. I think a friend of hers picked her up, and they drove into town together."

"What?! You mean she hasn't even *started* yet?" Lloyd was good and properly angry. Not unusual. Brian sighed. His brother-in-law would next do his typical huff and puff and eventually run out of steam when it mattered most. Brian rarely paid any attention to his blusters anymore.

"Listen, I got to get going here," Brian said. "Got a few things to do yet before supper. When you talk to Stacey, maybe get her to give me a call and let me know what's happening, okay?" Brian knew from past experience that he'd hear nothing back from either her or Lloyd, but he wisely kept that to himself. No sense in stirring up a shouting match. It had never worked to his benefit in the past.

"Yeah. Sure," Lloyd answered absently. Then he was gone.

Brian grinned foolishly. Why he felt a sense of victory, he wasn't at all sure. It seemed a guarantee that the housework wasn't going to get done in any fashion. For once though, he decided he wasn't about to bust his own hump doing something that had already been given to a young gun for hire who was supposedly super keen to make money. He wasn't picking up the slack this time. Enough was enough. No doubt, Louise would rant and complain about it in her own way when she got home. *Oh well, not my problem*, he conceded happily.

Leisurely, he stepped outside and noticed the weather changing. Looked like rain clouds trundling in. Going back into the garage, he pulled out the portable air compressor in order to reinflate Louise's car tire, which he'd purposely deflated some days back.

"Hey, Rufus, old buddy," he said to the grey cat now sitting patiently just inside the door. "What do you think, big guy? Just about time for a beer? Might even order a pizza. You like pepperoni, right?"

Rufus meowed his approval.

Aurora Magic

I OPENED THE BACK SCREEN DOOR as quietly as I could and looked around. Being a Saturday, the yard was busy with customers, but they were closer to the warehouse than the house. Stepping on the landing outside, I carefully leaned the door closed, and then tiptoed to the corner of the house, ready to bolt towards the street.

Her voice colourless, Mom's words stopped me cold. "Where are your brothers, Eunice? I thought they were going to the movies with you this week."

I froze, my heart hammering. Slowly turning around, my mind raced, trying to find a safe answer. Neatly hidden as she was behind the stacks of plywood immediately outside the back door, it was only as she stepped out into the open that she finally became visible.

Stepping around the edge of the wood pile, she slowly pulled off the well-worn work gloves she always wore in the yard, tucking them firmly under one arm. Then she pushed her hair away from her face, removed a bobby pin and reinserted it, catching several stray locks along the way.

"Answer me, girl. Do you want to lose your allowance? Is that it?" she said menacingly, moving closer.

You can't take my quarter! I thought in a frenzy, my fist tightly clutching the silver coin. Unconsciously, I started backing away, my hand hidden behind me.

"Ho, ho! Are you thinking that will save you? Are you? Well?"

"They told me they wanted to go to the store instead of the movies, so that's where they went," I finally blurted out. "I had to pee, and they wouldn't wait for me."

"You should have stopped them. That's your job," she stated, giving me a piercing look. "How many times have I told you they're too young to go to the five-and-dime alone?"

"I'll run and get them, okay?" I begged. "I'll bring them home."

"You know what happens when you don't listen to me, don't you?" she continued, looming over me. As I tried to edge away, she shook her head. "Don't you move."

I stopped. It would only get worse if I didn't listen. Of course, it got worse anyway. With a quick movement, she backhanded me across the side of the head. I wanted to cry out at the pain, but instead held it tight inside. Like always.

"I'll go right now, Mommy. Please, let me go!" I pleaded, and then just stood there waiting, completely still and uncertain what to do.

Without another word, she turned and walked towards the warehouse, casually slipping her gloves back on as she went.

I spun around then and ran as fast as I could the full three blocks to main street. Both boys were exiting the store just as I arrived. Each was grasping a small bulging paper sack loaded to the brim with candy. Donnie's mouth was already full of a huge gumball.

Panting heavily, I stopped right in front of them. Both of them totally ignored me. "Hey," I puffed, my breath coming out in a rush. I was kind of angry but more hurt than anything else. "Why didn't you guys wait for me? Huh?"

Donnie opened his mouth as if to speak, but instead of words, pink gum oozed out, which he quickly stuffed back in with two grimy fingers.

"Mommy said I have to bring you home right now!" I said in a rush, my tone stressing the urgency of the command.

Donnie glared at me while slowly pulling the sticky gob from his mouth. His chin went up as he said, "We don't want to go home. Do we, Ricky?" Glaring defiantly, he poked the messy wad back inside his mouth once more, wiping the residue on his fingers down the front of his t-shirt.

"No, we don't," said Ricky, mimicking Donnie's voice. Defiantly, he stuck out his tongue at me.

"You have to take us to the movies," Donnie declared sullenly, his words slurring. "That's what Mommy said."

"How much of your allowance do you have left?" I asked smugly. There would be none. Their bags said as much.

They shared a dismal look. Then Donnie shook his head, slowly deflating. "Nothing."

"Then you can't go," I stated flatly.

Their faces fell, and my smugness vanished. "I'll take you next Saturday," I said softly. "You just can't spend your allowance first. Okay?"

"I want to go to the movies *now!*" Ricky wailed, tears spilling from his eyes.

"Don't cry, Ricky," I said, my voice gentle now. "How about you show me what you bought? I'll bet I wish I had some of what you got there."

His lip continued quivering, though his tears were momentarily quelled as he eagerly opened his bag, allowing me to ogle his cache.

Both boys deliberately dawdled the entire trek back, but we finally arrived at home. I quickly deposited the pair of them at the sandbox by the side of the house, where they immediately plopped down, happily sorting through their candy horde. Fearful that my mother would find another reason to detain me, I tried to evade her scrutiny by racing down the back alleyway. She saw me and scowled. With customers milling about, there was little else she could do. But her face made it clear that there would be an accounting later. Pushing that thought aside, I kept running.

✳ ✳ ✳

THAT'S ALL THE PARTICULARS I remember from a single Saturday when I was about eight years old. If other memory snippets serve as evidence, it was probably a pretty typical day for me back then.

Not sure why this solitary chunk of remembrance has survived intact when so much of everything else resembles pulverized sawdust. Maybe it has to do with the fact that Saturdays were special to me. It was then that my younger brothers and I received our weekly allowance. Twenty-five cents each. A princely sum in the fifties.

Penny candy was exactly that, and "jawbreakers" were three for one. One cent was enough for a whole red licorice strip. Or a Double-Bubble gum cocooned inside a zany cartoon wrapper. Or even a single sugar strawberry. For two precious pennies, one had the choice of a thick black-licorice pipe or a cigar, the tips of both generously coated with red-candy sprinkles. A complete nickel could get you a slim slab of gooey, parchment-covered, tri-coloured KooKoo toffee. There were chocolate bars in two sizes: five cents and ten. Seven cents got you a double popsicle. A Revel ice-cream bar, Fudgsicle, or Drumstick fetched a whopping ten cents each. All were so tempting, but every week, my own piece of silver was destined for a grander fate.

Once received, it was just a matter of clock-watching. Shortly before two, down the alleyway I would run, past our warehouse stuffed with building materials and a stacked yard's hodgepodge of sawhorses, planks, and scaffolding. A slower jog was called for over the callused and uneven dirt path that ran parallel to the skating rink's weathered slats. This was followed by a diagonal dash over the first gravel roadway. Then across the nearest empty lot and down another alley and the sandy access boulevard separating creamery and bakery. Suddenly, a complete and abrupt halt.

Jaywalking Saturday's main-street traffic could be tricky. A lurching gridlock of frustrated drivers and tooting horns. All wishing for that miracle parking slot to open up along the crowded thoroughfare. A bit of cautious dodging through the vehicle line-up landed me safely on the sidewalk opposite just long enough to slip through the narrow gap between the ladies-wear shop and a squat one-story. The shortcut's wooden walkway ended at another laneway and the rear of the post office. Skirting down the side of that government edifice, and around the edge of the front lawn, and then there it was:

The Aurora Theatre!

I'd be smiling as I hurried down that sidewalk. Even unlit, the theatre's vertical neon signboard was a beacon, jutting jauntily out across the roofline and above the sidewalk. I generally cared little what the afternoon movie actually was. It was more important to just be there. That said, I still stared a full minute or more at the feature's mammoth billboard tacked snugly inside its plate-glass showcase.

Saturday afternoons, the theatre's entranceway was always jammed. A queue formed well before the doors opened, with a hubbub of voices, throngs of kids, animated chatter, laughter, and impatient glances towards the shuttered door. I remember it all. Bo Hodgson and a few of the older boys were usually early arrivals. Their inevitable scuffling and shoving generally secured Bo a prized spot at the front of the line. His hard-won victories won him the right to a solid grip on the front door's brushed-nickel handle. A few random parents often completed the perimeter of this energized jumble, which probably helped in keeping the noise and hullaballoo to a loud hum instead of a roar.

At two p.m. sharp, one half of the huge double doors swung abruptly outward. Those hovering nearest momentarily scattered. An usher immediately hustled out and inserted a wooden door-stop at the door's base before scuttling quickly back inside. Kids instantly poured through the opening only to be halted a few steps into the dimness. It was time to pay. The crowd inched ever inwards as coins clanked on the slender ledge that hugged the admission-booth window.

My quarter carefully placed was swiftly snatched up, and a slim dime plunked down in its place. Clasping the smaller circle of silver, I joined a second shuffling line. My gaze locked automatically on readied popcorn bags heaped on one side of the small snack counter. Greasy stains leaking through the white paper verified the generous dollops of butter inside. The scent heavenly, my mouth watered in anticipation of tasting it! Occasionally, my focus faltered, settling on licorice packets or assorted candy bars instead. Once or twice, I erred and chose one of these. On those instances, my yearning for the absent popcorn lingered well through the afternoon and even later. Each week, I reminded myself to never again repeat the blunder!

Clutching my coveted popcorn bag tightly, I joined the boister-ous rush into the seating area. Front row centre was the prized spot. I never made it that far but usually got close. Sort of. Second row, left aisle was generally the best I could do.

I wouldn't allow myself to unfold the top of the bag until the lights had dimmed, after what always seemed like an infinite amount of time, and the huge curtains parted. All babble stilled as the film began, my focus completely riveted on the screen.

First always came the inevitable news clips. Flickering scenes in black and white of adults meeting, shaking hands, nodding heads, or staring at the camera, all while a monotone voice droned on and on. Topics centred on such things as commodity prices *(huh?)*, global issues, sports, and stuff like that. A completely silly Looney Tunes cartoon followed. My favourite was always Bugs Bunny.

Then there would be a Three Stooges comedy clip. Though I had seen many of them more than once, somehow knowing what silliness was coming made them seem even funnier on each repeat. I laughed continuously at all the antics! Lots of laughter around me too. After that were previews of upcoming attractions. By this point, I would check my popcorn to ensure that there was enough to last through the main feature. Usually, it was half empty, which was a definite signal to slow down!

I don't actually recall a lot of specific movies or their plots. A few better than others. Whatever else happened during the course of the film, one thing was absolutely critical for me: At the movie's conclusion, the good guys had to win! Since that seemed to be the prescribed message of the movies from that era, I don't recall ever being disappointed.

The theatre was my refuge. Aurora's—as we called it—was an enchanted portal, within which I could safely blend into her cocooned darkness and interweave fantasies into the stories playing across that giant screen. My own "happily ever after," if you will.

All too soon, the movie was over. "The End" splashing across the final image on the screen before it faded to black, heavy curtains began closing, and theatre lights flashed on. Instantly, absolute madness and chaos erupted within a cacophony of shrieking voices, scrambling bodies, and thundering feet pounding through the marked exit corridors and into the alleyway beyond.

I was never ready for such an energetic exodus. Most times, I was one of the last stragglers out of the building, a harsh remainder of the day still ahead of me.

Yet, no matter what reality I had to deal with when arriving home, there was always one consistent ray of hope that carried me onward: *Only seven more sleeps until the next Aurora magic!*

Bright Skies

"What do you think of your folks still living in Bright Skies?" Gloria asked. "Have you ever talked to them about whether they'd consider living in another area of the city?"

Finally. Randy had been waiting nearly fifteen minutes, wondering when she'd get around to explaining her reason for stalking him on social media. He couldn't even remember who the heck she was, so he'd put feelers out to a few friends. The question, *"Who is Gloria Blacklock?"* drew quick responses: *"A realtor, bro."*

Hell, even Randy knew that much! If her name and photo on various bus benches and rolling billboards were any indication, she was a veritable celebrity in local real estate. Big hair and matching smile. That was her. It still didn't answer the question of why she was chasing *him* though.

Wow, he thought. *Bright Skies. That's way back.* Nobody called it that anymore. Now it was simply "the Bog," a moniker that spoke volumes.

If his parents' reminiscences meant anything, the place had been really hopping back in the early days. In the seventies and eighties. Young families. Vibrant communities. Successive generations moving out of the area, coupled with high-density housing consuming single-family lots, had since sent the area into a tailspin.

He remembered clearly St. Josaphat's. Elementary and junior high. Overcrowded. Bustling. Fun. Still couldn't place Gloria in the midst of that jumble, but then again, there were lots of kids there. Though he maintained connections with a few hangers-on, most had drifted away once high school had become a reality.

Since Gloria had managed a fancy jig around introducing her topic, Randy decided to do a two-step himself. Not willing to provide an adlib response, he took his time swallowing a mouthful of tepid coffee before asking his own question: "Why the interest?"

"Oh, nothing in particular." She shrugged, but Randy doubted its sincerity.

A quick initial assessment of her had told him a lot. Designer clothes. Jewelry. She was definitely monied. On the other hand, Randy knew that he was an easy read as blue collar. There was a time he'd dreamt of running his own plumbing shop, but over the years, he'd decided he was happy enough working for a local outfit. Figured he didn't need to be any higher up the food chain.

"So, do you keep in touch with anyone from the Phat?" he asked innocently, figuring that maybe there was an angle in that direction.

"No, not really,'" she replied in a tone that sounded a bit guarded.

Randy then launched into a brief rendition of newsy facts surrounding his old crowd, but Gloria soon interrupted.

"Listen, Randy, there actually is something I want to talk to you about."

"Oh, yeah?" he quipped, a bit annoyed at this point. "Listen, I got to get going here." He deliberately glanced at his watch. He'd had enough of this dance. Besides, his lunch hour was nearly over.

Gloria sighed. "You've probably noticed that Bright Skies is getting pretty beaten down. Do you think your parents would at least be willing to check out a new area? Have they mentioned anything? Maybe you could talk to them?"

Randy decided to be candid. "Mom might consider moving, but Dad has just settled into retirement. I'm guessing neither one of them is really keen about getting into mortgage payments this late in the game. Why?"

"Just working on some properties in and around Bright Skies, and the old days came to mind." She was clearly hedging. "Feeling a bit nostalgic, I guess. That's about it, really."

Randy knew he wasn't even close to hearing the truth but let it ride, abruptly deciding that he didn't want to hear any more. "I gotta go. I'm on the clock." As he stood up, Gloria slipped him a couple of business cards.

"Keep me in mind if they *do* decide to relocate, okay?" she said. "I've got some nice properties ready for move-in on the south end. Get them to give me a call."

Randy took the cards and jammed them into his jacket pocket. "Sure. No problem." He had no intention of doing any of that. Nodding *adios*, he hustled out to his truck.

✳ ✳ ✳

THE REST OF THE DAY, Randy couldn't stop thinking about the strange encounter. Immediately after work, he phoned his brother. "Hey,

Josh, can you meet me at Mom and Dad's tonight? I'd like to talk to them about something and want your input. I tried calling Elise, since she's always complaining that she's the last one 'in the know' on anything happening in the family, but I couldn't reach her."

"I'm guessing she's probably got something going on with one of the kids. Everything okay?" Josh asked, sounding slightly alarmed.

"Hope so," answered Randy distractedly, then swiftly added, "Sorry. Hadn't meant to sound like that. All's fine, far as I know. Just had a weird meet-up with a real-estate gal, and I'd like to hear their thoughts."

Randy arrived a minute or so before Josh. As they entered the side gate together and strolled to the back door, he filled his brother in on his meeting with Gloria. A couple of lights were on in the house as Randy rang the doorbell and entered the door code on the security panel.

"Hey, Mom? Dad?" he shouted, stepping into the foyer. Silence. Even Mutt, the Heinz 57, didn't respond. That meant only one thing.

"Garage," they said in unison, sharing a smile.

Slipping back outside, they walked through the evening coolness towards the building at the edge of the property. As they neared, Mutt began barking. *Better than an alarm,* thought Randy, grinning.

The large dog shook with delight at their appearance. A few pats, and he happily resettled himself on his comfy bed in the corner.

Glancing around, Randy couldn't help thinking, *What has Dad gone and done now?* Shaking his head, he shared a look of disbelief with his brother.

Earlier in the year, Gord Forrester had finally finished the restoration of a 1964 Chevelle Malibu SS that had started its rescue as an auction wreck. Countless hours of labour and more dollars than he meant to spend had eventually restored the baby-blue two-door to its original splendour. His initial intention had been to keep it for country summer drives when a chance encounter with a car buff from the coast had changed his mind. The substantial amount he'd offered was more than Gord could realistically turn down. After the sale, he'd stated repeatedly that he was finished resurrecting beaters. Period.

Yet, that was exactly what sat in the Chevy's former spot: a busted-up, rust bucket of a vehicle that looked like it could possibly have started its life as a 1960-something Chrysler Valiant.

"Good God, Dad!" Randy began, his voice echoing his incredulity. "This one's in even worse shape than the Malibu was!"

Josh was ambling slowly around the car's dilapidated perimeter, shaking his head. "It seriously is beyond a wreck."

Gord peered at them over his glasses before turning attention back to his task of removing the driver's door mirror. "And hello to you two. What are you guys doing here on a weeknight? One of you finally getting married or something?"

"Wow!" Josh exclaimed, his eyes widening at seeing a huge television mounted on an opposing wall, a muted football game being played on its screen. "You even got satellite out here now!"

"Hmph."

Randy ignored his father's grunt and looked around. Yup, the garage was a sturdy unit. Better built than the house. He knew that first-hand since it had been his, Josh, and Elise's unskilled hands that had helped complete the garage project years back. Under Dad's supervision and exacting standards, of course. No corners cut anywhere. Top-grade industrial wiring, a heated floor, and triple insulation, including the wide door for vehicles. No draft was ever coming in through that baby! A high-end security system completed the setup. No potential thief was going to easily wrangle Gord's hard-earned gear away from him. Not if *he* had anything to say about it!

Randy's eyes widened at seeing the recliner and sofa from the house's rec room, which had been resettled into one corner of the garage, along with two small tables and a full-size fridge.

Josh verbalized what Randy was thinking. "How come the mancave is out here now?"

Gord shrugged indifferently. "Your mom's been talking about wanting to turn that space into a craft room of sorts. Anyway, Saturday's game is coming up, and with Alec and Martin coming over, I just thought we'd watch it out here. Ended up getting the fridge for a real steal from a warehouse clear-out. Hey, there's sodas and brew in there, if you guys are interested. Help yourselves."

Randy pulled open the refrigerator door. Literally chock-a-block full. Munchies included.

"Whew! You're really loaded up in here! Mom allowing those snacks, is she? Thought she was pushing you to salads, veggies, and the like. Good ole healthy stuff," Randy joked, both he and Josh sharing a laugh at their father's expense.

Gord gave them a piercing look, then grimaced. "Okay, geez… I'm out here trying to get *away* from that kind of pestering."

"Where is Mom, anyway?" asked Randy.

"Out with Elise," Gord replied. "One of the grandkids has got something going on at the school. Should be home in an hour or so. Hell, guys, let's go in the house. I'm about done for today."

With Mutt running happily ahead, they left the garage, and Gord reset its alarm.

A HALF HOUR LATER, WITH a few general pleasantries out of the way, Gord gave them a shrewd look. "Okay, you two, what's up? Not that I don't appreciate the visit, but when both of you show up unannounced, I've got to wonder what the hell is going on. So? What the hell is going on?"

Josh looked at Randy, giving him the floor.

"Well," Randy began hesitatingly, "I know you've always said that you were only leaving this place 'boots first,' and by the look of everything, I'd say you haven't changed your mind. I still have to ask, though. Are you and Mom planning on selling?"

"Where did you get that notion?" Gord asked, looking hard at his two sons.

"I just had a chat with this realtor today—"

"Gloria, right?" Gord cut in. "Why the blazes did she talk to *you?*"

"Well, she was definitely on a selling pitch. That much was obvious. Now that I'm thinking about it, she was dodgy about everything. What gives with that?"

"Was wondering that myself after she showed up some days back," Gord replied, leaning back in his armchair. "From what I'd been gathering, she's making the rounds throughout the neighbourhood. Got a call from Gladys and Trent down the street, asking me if I had any idea what was going on. According to them, she came across pretty aggressive. The one interesting thing is that those she's contacting seem to be only original buyers from back in the seventies. Whatever she's doing though, one thing was pretty clear: She might not be saying it, but she's really pushing a move-out. The whole thing made me more than a bit curious." Gord paused then, deep in thought.

"And?" Randy wanted to know more.

"Sorry," Gord said, pulling himself from his reverie. "Was just remembering how we came to live here in the first place. A promo flyer in our mailbox, I think. It got your mom and me dreaming that maybe we could afford our own place. Bright Skies was already set up with paved streets, sidewalks, utilities, and the like. In talking to a few other old-timers, I was told this area had originally been peddled towards middle- to high-income families. Developers had been advertising it as 'upmarket housing.' Those people started balking, though, after small talk spiraled into serious concerns about the possibility of sink holes appearing on land that was basically reclaimed muskeg."

He sighed and went on. "The whole endeavour escalated into a real-estate nightmare. But hell, they still needed buyers, right? Too much had already been spent on infrastructure. Investors were getting antsy. So, they flipped tactics. What about leveraging low-income earners? Even though it wasn't the original plan, they were getting desperate. I remember a few eager-beaver real-estate guys roaming door to door through our rental units. At first, we didn't think we could afford it, but we listened. Long story short, we took the plunge. Lots of others bought into the same idea, with the end result being a bunch of cookie-cutter houses built on the cheap. We didn't care. What mattered was that we had our own place! Seriously awesome and hands down better than renting! All in all, we figured we got a pretty sweet deal."

"So, you're definitely not selling then?" Randy assumed.

Gord frowned. Letting out another sigh, his tone turned serious. "Almost everyone from the early years is gone. Things are changing, guys. Kinda hard to explain, really, unless you're living out here. It's just different. Lately, your mom and I had been tossing around the idea about possibly moving out, but that was all it was. Just talk."

"Whoa, whoa, whoa! What? You're selling?" Josh blurted, flabbergasted.

Gord looked from one son to the other. "Okay, okay. Your mom and I were going to discuss this with all you kids at the same time, but stuff kind of changed after Gloria showed up. Strange, that. She never really said anything but kept alluding back to when we first bought. Put a burr under my saddle. Decided to dig around. Went through our original sales agreement, and followed that up with checking a few things online. Even had Gene go over some of the legal jargon."

"Gene?" Randy said.

"Yeah, Gene Gowchuck. You must remember him…No? Been kind of the family lawyer since forever. Semi-retired now but keeps his hand in here and there. He found something interesting."

Gord paused, staring hard at one and then the other. "First off, I really have to thank that pesky gal. If not for her antics, I wouldn't have known what was going on."

"What's going on?" asked Randy, now totally enthralled, glancing at his brother, who wore the same look of anticipation. What could possibly be interesting about non-descript properties in a dead-end stick of the city?

"Well, Gene noticed a peculiar clause in our purchase agreement," Gord said. "Remember I told you developers were so eager to sell and couldn't get people interested? Because of that, they put in a caveat to make the area more appealing. No joke here, but it states specifically that if any sinkholes show up within the subdivision while the original buyer still owns the property, that buyer is entitled to a hefty pay-out."

"What?!" chorused Randy and Josh.

"Yeah," Gord continued, now excited and leaning forward in his chair. "The catch is that this only pertains to *original* owners who haven't sold. After so long, that clause was pretty much forgotten. I sure didn't remember it. Besides, most original owners are long gone now. There's not even a dozen of us left. I managed to round up most of us, and we had a little meeting. Gene was there too, bringing along another legal-beagle type to review what's what. It's been kept hush-hush, but there have been sinkhole issues close to Drover Road. Everything on the Q.T. Nothing in the media. Not yet anyway."

"Drover Road?" Randy said. "That's just a few blocks from here!"

"There's another bit too." Gord's voice turned grim. "It's all being kept quiet because someone clued into the existence of the handful of us original owners with that caveat in our purchase agreement."

"So, what happens now?" Josh asked.

"Well…" Gord shrugged, and then continued in a no-nonsense kind of way. "None of this is going to be easy, but we're pushing forward to see what's going to happen if and when the sinkhole problems become public. Though your mom and I *were* talking about maybe moving, now we're thinking we'll stick around till we see what happens with that. Don't want to lose out on receiving a chunk of money.

"Oh, and another bit," he added, "Gene accidentally discovered why this Gloria woman is so hell bent on people selling. It seems that her dad is the owner of Atomski Construction. You know them, right? The big development company involved in resuscitating the area, like that new golf course and fancy clubhouse on the east end of Bright Skies. From what Gene heard, the guy's a real jerk, and he and Gloria have been on the outs for years. Gene thinks maybe she's just trying to stick it to her old man. Seems that money is a pretty big deal with him, and she's just trying to get our sinkhole clause to bite him in the butt. Probably figured that, by acting like an overly pushy real-estate agent, she would get people talking and checking into stuff, including the forgotten clause. Gene's just guessing, of course, but it's as good a reason as any."

"Yeah," Randy said pensively. "Gloria Atomski…Sure. I kind of remember that name now. Is her brother named Arnold?"

"Could be." Gord shrugged.

"So, she's getting back at her pop," Josh said, shaking his head in disbelief and then reflectively lamenting. "With all of this, you know we've got a bigger problem to deal with, right?" He shot Randy a knowing look and got a smile in return.

Their father looked baffled now. "What are you talking about?"

"Elise," the brothers said simultaneously.

"What's your sister got to do with anything?"

"She's going to say that this is just another example on how she's never in the know about what's happening in the family," Randy said almost gleefully. "She's really going to have her panties in a twist on this one!"

Josh nodded, smiling, "Yup. You bet!"

"Uh…yeah. Well, it's not exactly like that," Gord offered sheepishly.

Randy looked puzzled. "Oh yeah? What is it like then?"

"Well…Elise was actually here when this Gloria dropped by. So she's actually known about everything from the get-go." He gave each of them a meaningful glance. "Seems it's you guys who are the last to know this time." He chuckled quietly.

"What?" the brothers shouted.

"Oh, God!" Randy groaned then. "We are *never* going to hear the end of this! Where's that beer you offered earlier? I think I'm going to need a few!"

Two for the Money

THE INTERIOR WAS WELCOMELY COOL as Evelyn stepped through the Mardi Gras Bistro's ornate entrance doors. It took only one quick glance to make her feel immediately underdressed in her t-shirt and frayed jeans. Never mind that the jeans were an outrageous $400—even on eBay!

Her gaze swept the sumptuous foyer that was housing no less than a dozen standing people awaiting table space. Undaunted, she strolled confidently up to a young blonde at the entrance podium, who was wearing platform heels and a micro mini. The name tag pinned to her blouse identified her as "Chantel."

"Good afternoon," Chantel began, her smile widening. "Do you have a reservation?" she asked, giving Evelyn the once over, and not kindly either.

"There should be one under Janey Turnbull," Evelyn replied frostily, glad that Janey had suggested making the reservation when they'd first connected online about her wedding and the possibility of Evelyn accepting the job of planning it.

"Ah, yes. I see it here. The other member of your party is already seated. This way, please." With that, the waifish figure led the way, somehow balancing easily on her three-inch stilettos.

Chatter was high in the dining area, a Friday lunch crowd filling the space. With a hasty glimpse around, Evelyn noticed the patio area was totally vacant, not surprising for midday in July. It was then that she realized this was exactly where she was being led! Outside past the French doors and beyond the air-conditioned bliss. Heat instantly enveloped her.

A few steps across the patio, Chantel stopped and cheerfully stated the obvious: "Here we are." She stepped aside to allow Evelyn to take her seat.

"Um…Are you sure it's—" Evelyn fell abruptly silent, freezing as she glanced at the woman already seated at the table, concealed under a wide-brimmed hat and dark glasses. It was someone she had hoped never to set eyes on again:

Liz.

Neither woman spoke.

Noting the uneasy silence, Chantel took advantage of it to awkwardly continue her default lines: "Todd will be your server today and will be along shortly to take your drink order. Have a lovely lunch, ladies." With that, she turned and swiftly skittered across the terrazzo tiles, disappearing back inside.

Evelyn broke the stillness. "What the hell are you doing here?" Scorn was practically dripping from each word.

The mouth beneath the tinted sunglasses smiled faintly. "Hello, Evelyn. You were expecting Janey, right? Well, I *could* tell you that she has decided to go with a different wedding planner entirely, but in truth...there *is* no Janey."

Evelyn's shock registered clearly in her expression. "What the hell is this?" she hissed. "You bitch! *You tricked me!?*"

"How else to get you here, huh?" Liz responded evenly. "I knew you could never resist a free lunch, especially at the splashiest new restaurant in the city. Besides, with this heat wave, we've got all the privacy in the world out here. So, park yourself, Evelyn. Down here under the umbrella is a lot better than standing out there roasting." Despite her words, her tone was working hard to imply complete indifference about where she chose to sit.

"I'm out of here!" Evelyn huffed in disgust, turning to go.

"I wouldn't do that if I were you," Liz cautioned icily. "Do yourself a favour, Evvie, and just sit down. Believe me. You'll want to hear what I have to say."

Evelyn prickled at the sound of the old nickname. Even as her nostrils flared slightly, she forced herself not to rise to the bait. With great reluctance, she sank down in the wicker armchair beneath the ample canopy.

Liz studied her intensely from across the table. "So," she began, her voice a lazy drawl, "how are you, Evvie?"

Evelyn suddenly couldn't restrain herself. "Stop calling me that! You know how much I hate that name!"

"Oh?" Liz said, goading her. "Let's get right to the point then; shall we?"

"What do you want, Liz?" Evelyn asked glibly. "To explain about ducking out in the middle of the night and leaving me on the hook for the following month's rent? I ended up having to move. Not nice,

Liz, what you did. Gone, just like *that.*" She snapped her fingers to illustrate her point.

"I have to admit," Liz agreed sagely, nodding her head in agreement, "that's how it could look to anyone who doesn't know the full story. But now we're going to chat about what *really* went down."

Evelyn sneered, and tauntingly asked, "What about *Sean?* Shouldn't he be here too?"

"Sean? I sincerely doubt you want that, Evvie. Besides, it's time to drop the act," Liz said harshly. "You see, I know everything, *including* how you did it." Her clipped words hung heavily in the space between them.

For the first time, a tingling fear trickled down Evelyn's spine. "It's too hot out here, and you're talking stupid," she said sharply. "I'm leaving."

"Alright. Go," Liz said quietly. "I thought maybe you and I could come to some sort of arrangement to help solve your dilemma, but there are other solutions, I suppose."

Evelyn's fear heightened. Her thoughts racing, she allowed herself to lean back, reluctantly conceding to listen to Liz's pitch. For now.

At that moment, a lanky young male entered the patio, balancing a tray loaded down with chilled glasses and a carafe of ice water.

Liz flashed him a brilliant smile. "This is marvelous! Thanks so much, Todd!"

"You're very welcome, miss. Would either of you ladies be interested in ordering additional beverages?" he asked, notepad in hand.

Smiling at Evelyn, Liz laconically said, "I'll order, shall I?"

Evelyn glared but said nothing.

Undeterred, Liz said simply, "A tall gin and ginger for the lady, and a Caesar for me, please. Oh, and Todd, we'll put off ordering lunch and just enjoy the sunshine for a bit."

Todd's eyebrows rose a notch at the suggestion that today's intense heat was something to be savoured, but aloud, he said only, "Sounds good. Your drinks will be out shortly."

As he left, Liz idly poured water and ice cubes into both glasses. Tipping her glass in a silent toast to her companion, she took a sip.

Ignoring Liz's gesture, Evelyn lunged for her water, greedily gulping a huge swallow before setting it back down. Her brain was racing wildly, and she found herself staring blankly at the glass, rivulets of condensation soaking into the napkin beneath. *This is totally asinine*, she thought. Opening her mouth to state exactly that, Liz interrupted, her voice flat.

"I almost feel sorry for you, Evelyn…Almost."

Evelyn was startled. "What are you talking about?"

Liz shrugged noncommittally. "You've always been so damn persuasive, but you know that, don't you? As an example, that huge apartment. You just had to have it. No way could I convince you that the rent was way above what we could afford, but did that sway you? *'Just need a spare roommate,'* you said. *'A few months, at best. It's easy. We can flip the den into a third bedroom and rent it out. We won't even need to inform the landlord.'* How I ever let you persuade me, I can't imagine now. And Sean? He was easily available to become that possible roommate. And both of you neatly omitted the little detail that it was the two of you who'd cooked up this scheme in the first place! That the *spare* roommate was always intended to be *me!*"

She stopped then, giving Evelyn a hard look. "I know you probably don't give a damn about any of this, Evelyn, but you're going to hear it anyway."

Evelyn scoffed loudly. "What are you doing here, Liz? Huh? This reminiscing? What are you trying to prove?" Snorting derisively, she stood up. "This is so typical of you! You're pathetic. You know that? I'm not listening to any more of this drivel!"

"You honestly didn't think you'd see me again, did you? Probably thought I'd just slink away, licking my wounds, and hoped I'd just fade away," Liz said coolly, giving Evelyn a level stare. "Maybe it'll be more productive for me to talk to Sean."

Sean. Evelyn's breathing quickened as genuine fear coursed through her, her mind racing. With no alternate plan at the ready, she sat back down and listened to Liz's bitter and meandering reminiscences.

"Where was I?" Liz continued, her tone easy and relaxed. "Oh, yeah. It didn't take long before I got a full sense of what I'd been suckered into. Should have seen it coming. It was always the same with you, but each time, I convinced myself that it would be different. Started almost as soon as we moved in too. The bathroom and kitchen always a mess. My clothes disappearing or ruined. Groceries pilfered. Typical Evelyn-style antics. I even tried locking stuff in suitcases for a while, but jimmying locks seems to be your specialty.

"Talking to you didn't work," she continued, "because what could I really do anyway? Hmm? My name was on that lease too. Finally, I got desperate. Had a fancy deadbolt installed on my bedroom door. That's when Sean lost it! I was leery of him from the beginning, but when he started his ranting, he really frightened me. Went on and on about me exaggerating everything, and ordered me to stop playing the injured diva, *'or else,'* Wasn't sure what he meant, but it freaked me out.

"By then, I had figured out that you and he were more than roommates. Still surprises me. The two of you. He wasn't the slippery useless type you're generally attracted to. For one thing, he had a job!" She paused, contemplating Evelyn's hate-filled glower. "Anyway, guess what happened next?"

Liz waited a moment, but Evelyn didn't take the bait. So, she went on, her tone one of almost chilling nonchalance. "A few days later, he comes to me, this time nice as can be. Needs a favour. Was thinking of asking you but wasn't sure if he could trust you."

Evelyn's mouth dropped. "You're lying, you witch! Sean would never—"

"Stop blustering, Evelyn!" Liz snapped. "He did! And that's that! So, for *once* in your life, just shut up and listen!" Her voice was tight with anger.

Startled, Evelyn did as she was told.

When Liz continued, her tone had softened somewhat. "So, it seems that he had been a part of a bastardized pyramid scheme that had just seen a hefty payout. The welcome cash was a bonus. Timing wasn't. Now, he had to figure out how to sidestep that windfall becoming entangled in his list of assets during his nasty divorce. With all his scamming going on, it just never crossed his mind that someone might pull one over on him!"

Evelyn's eyes widened. Liz paused, and taking a leisurely drink, noted her obvious discomfort. A small smile flitted across her face before disappearing as quickly as it had appeared.

At that moment, Todd stepped through the doorway and across the patio. With a smile, he deftly transferred two beverages from tray to table. Evelyn immediately dove for hers, taking a deep slurp.

Gallantly averting his gaze, he addressed Liz. "Will there be anything else?"

Studying Evelyn for a second, Liz said, "No. I think we're fine for the moment, Todd. Thank you, though."

He nodded and was gone.

Picking up her glass, Liz enjoyed a generous pull on the Caeser as Evelyn quietly studied her every move through narrowed eyes. After a long pause, during which she ignored Evelyn completely, she started speaking again in a thoughtful tone of voice, "Sean and his money...He reckoned I could just go to a bank and deposit it all under my name. *'No biggy,'* he says, but even I knew better than that. Banks can be damn suspicious about huge chunks of cash. So I laughingly say to him, *'Buy yourself a heavy-duty home safe, Sean.'* As a bonus, I even suggested he could bolt it to his bedroom floor. And what does he say? *'Sure!'* He actually agrees with me. Thinks it's a great idea! Goes me one further though. Tells me the safe's going in *my* room, since I have a deadbolt on my door.

"Et Voila!" Liz took another cooling sip of her beverage before continuing. "Suddenly, there's a safe in my room. He plunks his

money inside it, sets the combination, and that's that. I was now the one left worrying about a surprise inspection from the landlord!"

Giving Evelyn a penetrating stare, Liz raised her glass again to her tablemate. "I have to hand it to you," she said dryly. "It took me a while to figure out how you'd found out about the safe itself, not to mention the money. For sure, it wasn't from Sean. That guy's paranoid about everything, and I'd never told a soul. It was when I remembered the circumstances of Sean giving me the safe's combination that I finally put it all together."

She stopped a moment, shaking her head in amazement. "One night, I'm having a bath, totally minding my own business, and guess what? Sean strolls right on in! I'm getting all embarrassed and frantically trying to cover myself, and all the while, he's laughing and joking that I haven't got anything he hasn't seen better somewhere else! What a guy, yeah? He gets to the point right quick, though. Tells me his boss has him working out of town for a bit, which gets him worrying about his money in case there's a fire. I remind him that the safe is guaranteed fireproof, but does he listen? Of course not. Instead, he tells me the combination, knowing I'm way too lily-livered to ever think about crossing him.

"At this point, I'm so concerned about getting him out of the bathroom that I totally forget how paper thin the walls in that apartment are. It's only later, when I'm trying to figure out how his money could have disappeared, that I remembered. You overheard everything, didn't you, Evvie? There was no one else who could have. And naturally, once you had the combination, it was just a matter of pilfering my deadbolt key. All in all, a bit risky, but when it comes to money, you always find a way, don't you?"

She paused, pursing her lips thoughtfully as Evelyn stared back at her, trying to appear unfazed. "Something else I thought about too, Evvie. It must have rubbed you raw, him trusting me like that instead of you. I think you wanted to get back at both of us." Leaning slightly across the table, she added in a low tone, "But there are two things you should have known before making the choice that you did, the first being to identify the true target you'd be stealing from, in this case, Sean. And the second is a saying— one that you seem unfamiliar with."

She tilted her head to one side and looked condescendingly at Evelyn. "Has no one ever explained to you that revenge is like ice cream? Best served cold?"

With a slight smile, Liz leaned back, observing Evelyn for a long moment as she fidgeted in her chair. Then she continued, her tone musing now. "Anyway, Sean's money went missing, of course. Several thousand, according to him."

Liz seemed to be studying Evelyn for a secondary reaction. There was none. Taking a deep breath, her tone shifted into one of barely constrained anger now. "You didn't step forward!" she spat. "Not even when he said he was going to beat me senseless if I didn't return it! *'Every penny and pronto!'* I was crying and swearing to him that I hadn't done anything, but then he threatened to call the cops and have me arrested!"

Scowling fiercely now, Liz added, "I didn't 'duck out' on the rent, Evvie. I panicked and ran, but you knew that, didn't you? I went into hiding, and I've been in hiding ever since…I even had to quit my job, but you don't care about that either."

Liz fell briefly silent then, taking a deep breath and exhaling slowly as she observed Evelyn closely. Leveling her next words with as much cutting clarity as possible, while trying to control her own emotions, she shook her head and asked, "Don't you have anything to say after what you put me through? Anything at all?"

Evelyn shrugged and directed a cold look at Liz. "Okay, yeah. I took the money. So what? He deserved it for treating me like one of his floozies! Besides, who better to take the fall than you? Boohoo, poor little Lizzie, huh? Is that what you were hoping I was going to say? That I'd confess and say sorry? Well, I'm going to have to disappoint you on that score, little sist—"

"Don't you dare, Evelyn!" Liz barked, her voice tight with rage. "Don't you *dare*, for even one instant, remind me that we are actually sisters! You have *always* played me, our whole lives, but never *anything* like that! I came here today with the full intent of helping you squirm out from under your own mess, but I'm done. Just so you know, I've actually already met up with Sean, to try and convince him to let me talk to you and figure out—"

"What?!" Evelyn shrieked as soon as she was able to find her voice, cutting off whatever her sister had been planning to say next. "You went to Sean?! Are you *bloody mental?* What the hell have you done to me?!" She jumped up then, her eyes wide with fear.

Liz just stared, momentarily dumbfounded, and then continued, her voice flat and emotionless now. "You know something? I think I'm just now realizing that you really don't give a damn about what happens to me at all; do you? Can you even hazard a guess at what his reaction to seeing me was?"

After a moment of non-responsive silence from Evelyn, Liz removed her hat and glasses. Evelyn gasped. Even carefully applied makeup couldn't fully conceal the black eye and considerable facial swelling and bruising.

"When I told him I wanted to help you, he laughed—" Her voice broke, and it took a moment before she could continue. "He seriously laughed out loud. Even called me a chump, especially when I said that all I wanted to hear from you was that you were sorry. Said that was never going to happen. That you're *'not wired that way.'* Boy, does he have you pegged!" She shook her head sadly. "How did I never see that?"

Crying quietly now, her tears carving thin trails through her makeup, which was pancaking in the heat, Liz redonned her hat and sunglasses. Then in a cold, disinterested voice, she added, "You can talk to him yourself. He'll be right out."

Evelyn gasped loudly. "Sean's here?!" She leapt to her feet and started sprinting towards the patio's fence.

"Evelyn, stop! You can't get away!"

Stopping on a dime, she swiveled around fast, features twisting in terror as she ran back to her sister. "Liz, you have to help me!" she pleaded. "Please, Lizzie! *Please!* You've got to do something!" Panicked tears started rolling down her face as she made a grab at Liz's arm.

Evading her grasp, Liz shouted, "What do you think I've been trying to *do* here, Evelyn?!"

At that moment, Sean burst through the French doors and out onto the patio. "Hey, girl," he said menacingly, striding quickly towards them, his attention focused solely on Evelyn, and then bellowing, "We need to talk and right bloody now!"

Evelyn pushed Liz roughly aside, wiping her cheeks suddenly and rearranging her features into an expression of pure joy as she rushed eagerly towards him. "Sean! It's so great to see you!" she gushed, excitely. "Liz just told me you were actually in the restaurant, and I couldn't believe it! I've been wanting to talk to you for *months* about this fabulous little wedding-planner company I invested your money in. Wanted to make sure it was making a decent profit before I surprised you with it. It's just starting to make some real money now, so it's absolutely *perfect* that you're here! Do you have time to talk about it right now or are you in a rush?"

"Uh…" Sean looked completely thrown by this. "But Liz said…" Bewildered, he shook his head. "Liz told me that—"

"Forget Liz," said Evelyn, her voice animated and trilling cheerfully as she subtly worked to steer him towards the table. "She never gets anything right. We both know that. How about you and me start with a couple of drinks, and then lunch? My treat. I'll fill you in on how everything's going. How does that sound?"

"So…you're saying that this company's making money? Is that right? How much are we talking here?" Sean was still puzzled but slowly becoming intrigued. He settled himself in the chair that had been vacated by Liz during the commotion.

"I'll fill you in on everything!" Evelyn exclaimed, her enthusiasm and excited chatter seemingly boundless.

Liz's initial disbelief at the spectacle playing out before her suddenly felt laughable. "Wow," she mumbled quietly. "The con and the conned. Perfect!"

With a wry grin, followed by a shake of her head, she left them to their own devices and headed out, with neither Evelyn nor Sean any the wiser.

Cat's Pyjamas

I WAS NOTHING. WOULD ALWAYS BE nothing. Was told that ever since I was little. Grew up believing it.

'Til one day…

* * *

IT WAS SNOWING. IT HAD started early. One of those freak October storms that takes everyone by surprise. Monkey was at his job as mechanic at the garage in town, Karl was on the sofa, daytime TV on, and Dorrie was working her usual shift at the café. I was glad anytime she wasn't around. A full-time bee-yach with a capital B is what I'm telling you. She was really pretty. I'll give her that. A head-turner. Under that shiny topcoat, cruel to the bone. But hey, that's another story.

Anyway, on that snowy day, she and Monkey left for work together before dawn in Dorrie's red Camaro. As rusted as it was, it still ran. Of course, Monkey had a lot to do with that. He could fix anything.

Karl had come off shift from the plant and gotten home at about the same time that Monkey and Dorrie were getting ready to leave. I could hear all three of them in the kitchen, yakking loud about nothing, none of them caring whether or not I was still asleep. The outside door slammed not long after, with the car starting up and pulling away. I listened 'til I couldn't hear it anymore. I also heard the sounds of the fridge door, a bottle being cracked open, and its cap hitting the floor.

Karl having a beer this early meant he was working another late slot tonight. Had to get the drinking in while he could, I guess. With him already boozing, it meant that I'd have to be a little more careful about staying out of his way.

I should explain. We all lived together in a junk of a trailer set about a hundred yards back of Karl's parents' house. Someone had ditched it at their farm years earlier. When Karl had decided to live on his own, the trailer was about as far as he'd felt like going at the time. Monkey had moved in shortly after. Can't be sure when Dorrie had been installed because Karl went through girlfriends like water through a sieve.

It's probably time to say something about Jonnie and me. I want to make it real clear that I hadn't "left home" because of him. I'd been kicked out. Ugly talk, fighting, beatings even. That was home. It was all I'd ever known. Still, I'd thought it better than nothing. Mama and Pa started grousing on about the fact I was getting too wild. Staying out late. Partying. Poor choice of friends. Don't know if I was wilder than any other teenager of the day. Maybe. Drinking a bit too. For a while, at least. My favourite had been lemon gin. Not because I liked the taste. Nasty stuff, that. But it was cheap. The downside was after only a couple of mouthfuls, I would be basically sloshed.

I'd decided right quick that drinking wasn't for me because what always followed was a lot of puking and feeling sick most of the next day. Anyway, when I was punted to the street, I'd only had about thirty bucks in my jeans, from babysitting. Couldn't waste it on drink. Scary being alone like that at fifteen. Probably why I hooked up with Jonnie right away, convinced he was my happy forever guy. I'd like to say he treated me better than my folks, but that might be stretching it. As long as I did whatever he said, things were great. So I learned to do that. At first we'd lived in this dump of an apartment, but I couldn't handle the bugs and mice. That's how we'd ended up at Karl's.

Karl and Monkey had jury-rigged the electrical at the trailer, connecting it to the house, before we ever got there. One thing the trailer didn't have was indoor plumbing. Only an outhouse. I hated it, especially at night. Karl's family let him and Dorrie use the bathroom at the house. The rest of us didn't rate. In the beginning, it had been Dorrie and me hauling water, doing dishes, and stuff. That had changed fast, though, when she saw that she could leave it all for me because I would do it anyway.

One important thing to mention here: I was pregnant, about seven or eight months, by the day of the big snowfall. Jonnie had been stunned when I'd first told him. Almost like he couldn't figure out how the heck that had happened. Seemed happy enough though, or so I'd thought. He'd proved me wrong. Took off as soon as I started to show. Decided he wasn't daddy material, I suppose. I'd thought I would miss him but didn't. It actually felt nice not having him yelling about something or other all the time. I phoned home right about then. Straight up thought that maybe I could go back. Told Mama about Baby. Still remember her answer: *"Just about what I expected from you, Ruby. Nothing but a tramp."* Then she'd hung up. For a lotta nights after that, I'd cried myself to sleep.

So there I was: sixteen, pregnant, and living with people who would rather I just disappeared. They'd never said that to my face, of course. I think they were a little afraid of Jonnie…just in case he came back. Generally, they let me be. Probably also liked it that I did most all of the cooking and cleaning!

Back to the snow day.

A few more hours passed, and Karl was still on the beer. I thought it dumb of him to drink, knowing full well he'd be working heavy machinery later, when he would more than likely still be half-drunk. That day, though, I made the mistake of saying that out loud, jokingly adding, "Not giving you any more beer!"

That's when he snapped. Went right off his nut!

He jumped off the sofa and started staggering around. Grabbed Cat by the scruff of his neck, and then with poor old Cat dangling in mid-air, he stumbled over to the kitchen counter and snatched up the butcher knife.

"How would you like it if I slice this old cat up, huh?" he yelled, spit and slobber running from his mouth. "What would you say to that?!"

I wanted to scream but kind of froze instead. That's how scared I was that he would really do it. "No, please, no!" I started crying. "I'll get you the beer! As many as you want! Please don't hurt Cat!"

Couldn't bear the thought. I loved him so much. He had been nothing but a yard cat, wandering around outside and eating whatever scraps he could find, but I'd made him mine when Jonnie left. The idea of being alone had been too much to take. One look at Cat and you could tell he'd had a hard life, with a piece missing from one ear and a huge scar on his backside where the fur never quite grew back. At first he didn't seem to know if he liked being inside, but he definitely loved being fed regular. Usually, I kept him safe in the bedroom with me. But not that day.

Karl looked at me through bloodshot eyes, I think trying to figure how much of a threat I was. Finally, he stumbled, dropping both Cat and the knife on the floor. Cat scooted away into my bedroom right away, and I shut the door fast behind him.

Swearing and mumbling, Karl fumbled his way back to the sofa while I hid the knife under some towels in a cupboard. I hurried to the fridge, got him a beer, and opened it. "Just how you like it," I kept saying. "Fresh and cold." Then another. And another. I don't know how many times I got him a fresh beer, but in between, I huddled at the far edge of the kitchen and as far away from him as I could get. Mercifully, however long it took, he finally passed out, the TV blaring some kind of wrestling match.

That's when I got mad. Boiling. First time in my life I ever got that worked up. He would have killed Cat. In a heartbeat. No doubt about it. A defenseless scrub of a cat who was doing nothing! Nothing at all!

I sat myself down and had me my first deep think. It took no time at all deciding what was happening next: Cat and I were leaving, and that was that. I went to the hidey-hole I'd fashioned for myself in the bedroom, pulling out the little travel bag I had pushed in there. It was the one I'd arrived with, containing my few clothes and bits of makeup. I stuffed in some undies, a couple of Jonnie's old shirts, and a second pair of his jeans he'd left behind. There were only two that still fit me. The ones I was wearing were held together at the top by a shoelace because the zipper wouldn't do up more than halfway anymore.

I was taking Monkey's Ford Galaxie. "Borrowing" is what I wrote in the note. Said I'd get it back to him. Didn't know how yet but wasn't going to think on that 'til later. With Karl's folks away in the city, this was about as perfect a day as I was going to get. Except for the weather.

There was one other thing: Aunt Vee didn't know I was coming. She wasn't even my aunt, but she had always been nice to us kids. Brought over candy and treats. Used to be friends with Mama. Had some kind of bust-up, with Aunt Vee even moving out of town. She lived over in Weston now and was the only person I could think to turn to. I had it sorted that I could find her easy enough once I got there. A town that size probably didn't have more than one hair salon anyway. Maybe two.

Karl moaning from the sofa got me moving quicker. Wiping a thick layer of snow off the car, I stuffed my bag in and plunked Cat on the passenger seat on top of a blanket I'd spread out for him. He lay down, quiet-like, almost as if he knew how important this was. On the other hand, Baby was kicking up a real fuss!

With the snow plastering my face, I looked up to heaven, praying for God to keep us safe. Then finally, I settled myself behind the wheel and noticed something that made me smile. I'd forgotten that the Galaxie was a four-speed! Reminded me of when I was about ten or so and driving lunch out to the men in the field. Pa had taught me how to work the stick, and though it was a little tough reaching the pedals at the time, that whole summer had been one of the happiest times of my life.

The trick with me driving on an actual road was that I didn't have a license. A learner's, yeah, but that doesn't count for squat without a licensed driver in the car. I shook off worrying what would happen if a cop pulled me over.

With the sky socked in low, it seemed later than it was. Had to get out of there before Monkey and Dorrie came home. Switched on the wipers and watched them scrape the newest layer of snow off the glass. I pressed in the clutch, slipped into first, and while releasing the pedal, eased on the gas. As slick as that, I rolled that ride right out of the yard, only turning the headlights on once I was past the house. I kept imagining Karl running out the door screaming, or his folks suddenly coming home. Neither happened. I checked the fuel. Nearly full. *Thank you, Monkey!* I only had about twenty bucks in chump change that I'd managed to cobble together over the past months and crossed my fingers it would be enough to get us there. I'd have to stop somewhere and get something for Cat and me to eat though. I was already hungry but trying not to think about it.

On a good day, Weston was at least a solid two-hour drive. Today, probably three or even more. I'd have to dodge the main highway for a few miles too since it passed right through the middle of town. Couldn't risk Monkey or Dorrie seeing the car. I'd be hooped six ways sideways if that happened. There was nothing for it but to take Old Road for a bit. *Damn.*

It was pretty nigh darkish when I turned off the local road and onto the old highway. Right off, I started ploughing through fresh snow that hadn't seen any traffic. The car started skidding around. From the get-go, I wondered if this wasn't going to be one of the big mistakes of my life. If I got stuck or slipped into the ditch, there was no one to help. Shivering, I turned on the heat. Cat seemed to soak in that warmth coming at him from the dash vent. Made me laugh, thinking that maybe his fur coat was just for show!

I drove real slow, focusing on not missing the bent stop sign at the fork. Had to take a left there to get me to the highway. Even with keeping an eye out for it, I almost didn't see it. The post was bent nearly clean over on its side. Less than a half hour later, I hit the main road.

Now I had another problem. Had to pee. A few miles on, I pulled off at a small stand-alone service station, petrified someone there might recognize the car. Or me. By then, I was worrying about everything! Bought a chocolate bar and a tin of cat food. Cost more than I wanted to spend, but we still needed to eat. Didn't come to me 'til later that I didn't even have a can opener. How dumb was that?!

There wasn't as much traffic as I thought there would be. Made it easier to drive slower than the posted sixty. There were still crazies though. Pickups and semis mostly, zipping by me like they were on fire. When they did, a whole mess of slop pitched across my windscreen. For a second or so, I'd be near blind 'til the wipers slapped it off. My heart was pounding like a jackhammer. That's what it felt like. I was so hungry but didn't know how to get the wrapper peeled off the chocolate with both my hands practically glued to the wheel. Besides, it was all the food I had, so best to hold off. I checked the gas gauge from time to time. Went down faster than I expected. Nothing I could do about that.

Sometime later, another service-station pitstop. Had a couple gallons gas spritzed in. Ate a bit of the chocolate. By then, I was more scared of running out of money for gas than for food.

We kept on motoring. I wanted to listen to the radio at one point, maybe some music, but didn't want to take my eyes off the road fiddling with buttons and such. Cat mostly slept.

In between all that, the snow kept coming and coming.

Then all of a sudden, a sign reading "Welcome to Weston" came into sight. The town's lights showed up shortly after. For the first time, I started to relax.

I stopped at a small grocery store long enough to ask if anyone knew where Viola Maxwell lived. Got puzzled looks until I mentioned, "She usually goes by Vee."

Right away, some lady with super red hair laughed. "Of course!" She gave me directions.

* * *

WITH FALLING SNOW STILL OBSCURING the distance like a heavy curtain, I pulled up in front of Aunt Vee's. It was then that I had another think. What if she slammed the door in my face, and I had to spend the night in the car? The thought sucked. Kind of shut my brain down quick on that thinking. One thing for sure. I was never going back to that trailer.

I decided I might as well get on with it and let Aunt Vee see everything that had just landed on her stoop. I stepped out of the car, sinking nearly knee-deep in snow. Stomped around to the passenger side, opened the door, picked up Cat, and wrapped him quick in a blanket. Couldn't risk him getting away. Then I walked up that snow-covered sidewalk, cold, hungry, and more than a little afraid.

It was a big old house with a couple of flowerpots on the small front veranda. Looked like they'd been cleaned up and made ready for winter. A good sign. Meant she was tidy and organized, or at least that's how I read it.

My heart thudding, I rang the bell. Heard footsteps. The outside light flicked on. Door pinched open, and there she was, kind of peering around one edge. Suspicious-like.

"Hi, Aunt Vee," I said, my mouth suddenly drier than a popcorn fart. "It's me, Ruby." I couldn't think of anything else to say. Hadn't rehearsed this part. I got so scared that I started shaking. What the hell had been going through my head, deciding this was a good idea?

Then her face broke into the hugest Aunt Vee grin, and she threw the door open wide. "Ruby? Oh, my God! Oh, my…" She kind of blubbered as her eyes ran over the whole package before her: Cat. Baby. Me. Everything.

I was holding my breath.

Stepping outside in slippers and track suit, she wrapped her arms around all three of us. Standing back a bit, and shaking her head with misty eyes, she said, "Well, if this ain't just the cat's pyjamas!"

I couldn't help but smile. It was what she always said when all was right in her world! Maybe I'd finally found a place where I wouldn't be afraid anymore…where I wouldn't be nothing.

That was something else I'd been churning through on the drive, slowly coming to the realisation that I was definitely not that. Not nothing! If Aunt Vee's didn't pan out, I wasn't going to just tough my way through like I'd always done with everything. I was going to be a mama soon. Baby *deserved* a good mama. I made a pledge then. A right and proper one too. Between God and me. No matter what it took, and whatever I had to do, no one was ever going to hurt me or mine. Not ever and never again.

And with God watching, in all the days that followed, I worked hard to keep that promise front, centre, and focused.

But that's another story...

The Hatbox Case

"MR. STAFFORD, I WOULD LIKE to hire you to do something only...*slightly* illegal."

Gerald Arthur Stafford, aka Gas, was startled. Since little surprised him anymore, the lady before him categorically merited a second look.

Gwen Wyler was probably in her mid-thirties with dark eyes and hair. Her austere grey business suit was paired with opaque stockings and flat shoes. A thin leather pocketbook lay flat on her lap as she sat stiff-backed on the edge of the visitor's chair. Though attempting to disguise it, she was clearly agitated.

"I don't know what you think investigators do," he stated, brusquely, "but I'm personally not comfortable performing tasks outside the confines of the law."

"I was given to understand you need the money," she noted smugly.

That singular statement decided him. He didn't like her. Never mind that she was here on the recommendation of a good friend. The words stung and had been said without any apparent concern over how they might be received. The fact she was right didn't make the statement any more palatable.

Though a part of his brain urged him to bid her a quick goodbye, his curiosity was too strong, and he decided to hear her out.

"Go on," he said simply, leaning back in his chair and observing her closely.

"First of all, Mr. Stafford, let me start again," she said, her tone reflecting an attempt at civility. "I didn't approach this request in the proper manner. I am not in the habit of asking people to break the law for me," she offered, attempting a smile she didn't quite carry off. Her chin trembling slightly now, she continued. "Indeed, if I had the courage, I would do this myself."

She was playing him. That much was clear. Nevertheless, he waited quietly for more information. Experience had taught Gas that most people felt compelled to fill awkward silences with words. Gwen Wyler was no exception.

"I don't know how much you feel you need to know before you agree to my request," she continued, tentatively, "but I imagine *this* might go a long way in convincing you." She opened her purse and extracted an envelope. With only the briefest of hesitations, she leaned forward and set it carefully down on his desk before resuming her rigid pose.

Gas picked it up. A quick glance and a flick through the bills inside were followed by a sharp intake of breath and renewed scrutiny of his visitor.

"Not enough?" she asked, somewhat surprised.

Gas smiled, at first reluctantly, though it broadened quick. "Who is it you want done away with?" he joked. Realizing his comment hadn't echoed with his intended jocularity, he added, "Sorry. Just a joke. What is it you want done?"

For the first time, her shoulders relaxed.

* * *

TWENTY-SEVEN YEARS ON THE POLICE force of a mid-size prairie city had found Gas ill-prepared for retirement. Two divorces had leveled his pension, thereby stretching already limited resources. He'd spent considerable time attempting alternate forms of employment, such as house painter, yard maintenance, and handyman, just to name a few. Unfortunately, a leg injury sustained years earlier had begun to wreak havoc. Put simply, he could no longer spend long hours on his feet. What he needed was a desk job. After considerable deliberation, he'd decided to resuscitate the investigative skills he'd gained while on the police force. With this thought firmly entrenched, he'd opened Stafford Seek and Find.

Initially, his clientele had been made up primarily of family members and a few friends, with both sources eventually branching into occasional referrals. Research requests centred primarily around family histories, certified business and property records, academic credentials, and the like. Gas was the first to admit that delving into mundane archival data might seem like the perfect recipe for monotony. To his astonishment though, he discovered it to be both exhilarating and fascinating!

Many search results could actually be scored online. Educating himself on the intricacies of an utterly alien tech-savvy environment took more time than Gas anticipated. Eventually, however, he became relatively adept at navigating the seemingly endless flow of information and landing on an authentic result. Still, there remained a robust supply chain of actual paper and microfiche files that hadn't yet made the move to digital. The reason was simple: a lack of public funds dedicated towards digitalizing the past. This meant actual physical legwork into regional government agencies and city registries, resulting in the inevitable exhaustive examinations of well-thumbed card catalogues and musty reference texts. It was federal government archives that proved the most daunting. Also, the least likely avenue from which to resurrect information. Gas declared repetitively that the deceased were afforded one luxury through federal annals that the living could never hope to achieve: complete confidentiality of their personal data!

✳ ✳ ✳

AFTER MS. WYLER LEFT, GAS found himself sitting very still in his chair, eyes firmly closed. Her request had been direct and straight-forward, even as he replayed her words over and over in his mind:

"I want you to go to my former employer's house and retrieve a personal item. An old-fashioned black hatbox on the top shelf of a basement closet. There are only memorabilia items inside, but they mean a lot to me. I was going to reclaim the case myself, but he was extremely angry when I resigned on short notice. Because of this, I have no wish to face him. Besides, he would destroy everything immediately if he realized I'd left something behind. Therefore, I'm adamant that you do not approach him directly."

Sounded simple. Sort of. Gas had learned the hard way that the obvious was most often something else entirely. Her overly generous payment was the biggest red flag. A thousand dollars to retrieve an old box? Dubious at best. Even to Gas. All in all, what it really came down to was that it would involve a break-in. Never mind that it was her personal property he was retrieving. He hadn't said no and was now wondering why. Maybe it was that bit of mystery that had intrigued him. Or maybe it was just the money.

He sighed.

I probably should have insisted on being paid upfront.

* * *

"CAN I ASK YOU SOMETHING?" asked Gas, a tad insecure at approaching his first wife for assistance.

Bella laughed softly. "I knew there was more to you wanting to meet for tea than talking about kids and grandkids. Checking in on them, as it were. Not like you at all, Gas."

He was a little taken aback. He felt sure—well, *somewhat* sure—that he visited with the kids often enough. Occasionally, at least. Bella's raised eyebrows and knowing look said otherwise. He filed that thought away to think more on later.

"I would like your opinion and your…clarity? I guess? You always look at situations clear on and can pretty much always pick up on things I've missed."

Bella's small smile of victory wasn't lost on Gas, though he wisely remained silent on the subject. "Go ahead," she said. "I'll try."

"It's to do with a client. I can't quite get a read on her." With that, Gas filled her in on Gwen Wyler's strange request.

"Just so I'm understanding this correctly," she began thoughtfully, "this woman is willing to pay you a thousand dollars to steal a box of her old stuff from the basement closet of a former employer because he won't give it up, even if requested. Have I got that right?"

"Yeah." Hearing this sensible assessment made him start viewing the odd petition in an alternate light. "What do you think?" he added unnecessarily.

They shared a glance, realizing they were on the same page, which she then summarized in a single word: "Bull."

* * *

THE NEXT FEW DAYS SAW Gas wrapped up in finishing off a couple other jobs, with Gwen Wyler's dilemma being given only an iota of thought, subconsciously dismissing its apparent importance to his new client. The fact that she was toying with him likely figuring more strongly in his choice to drag his feet than he was willing to admit.

He focused instead on two archival searches nearing completion. The first was for a distant cousin attempting to attain Belgian resident status through ancestry. *No doubt wanting legal access to the European Economic Union,* thought Gas. There was also the separate case of a husband and wife who were trying to ascertain if the rejection of their business-license renewal was entirely legal, given that the city was intending to build a posh sports stadium nearby. Both research cases were leaning rather heavily towards negative results for his clients.

Suddenly, feeling very disillusioned for his cousin and the business owners, he found himself sighing defeatedly. *Damn,* he thought, feeling dejected. Craving a cigarette, though not quite enough to descend the staircase and go outside to have one, he just sat there, his frustration growing. Gwen Wyler popped back into his mind, as did Bella's concise appraisal.

"Bull," he found himself saying aloud. Then he grabbed keys, smokes, and glasses and was off.

* * *

THE HOUSE WAS IN ONE of the more seasoned areas of town. "Seasoned" as in nurtured, maintained, and tucked away from nearby neighbourhoods by a heavily foliaged parkland. These homes had been built on one-acre parcels, unlike the newer ones being set on lots that were quite skimpy by city standards. When he was a kid, the area had been referred to as "ritzy." He found that it had weathered rather well over the decades, still retaining that solid, respectable feel. Much of the architecture, as well as the layout of the properties, resembled English manors, a historical detail that tantalized him. *Something to check into further*, he thought. In any case, suffice it to say that there was money and lineage in Auburn Estates.

Number 21 had a circular drive, the blooms and abundant shrubbery surrounding it absolutely breathtaking. Then he remembered something. Wasn't this the address that had won first place for the best city-front garden last summer? Absently, he found himself wondering if it was in competition for this year's honour as well.

Leaving his car on the street, he strolled up the drive, admiring the view. He had long since determined what he *wouldn't* do. Now though, it suddenly dawned on him what he *would*. Without a further thought, he rang the bell.

*   *   *

"It's about time you got back to me! What took you so long?" demanded Ms. Wyler in a thickly accusatory tone.

"I *do* have other clients," Gas replied evasively, "though I have to admit, your request was rather intriguing. The money was the clincher. Of course, you knew it would be, though you were wrong about the reason. It was the amount offered for the job you described that really fascinated. *Way* too much for the return of an old hatbox full of trinkets. That was your mistake, Ms. Wyler."

He paused briefly, noting that she was now looking at him the way a caged animal looks at its handler. Then he casually added, "I did manage to secure the box though."

"What?" Her eyes widened briefly. "Well, where is it?" she practically snarled, her eyes darting about and taking in every corner of Gas's office.

"Right here," he said, pulling it out from beneath his desk and placing the battered box on its surface between them, patting its circular lid. "There you go."

Her eyes narrowed immediately at the box's lock, which had clearly been tampered with, and then she gave him a wary look. Grabbing it with both hands, as if expecting it to be quite heavy, she savagely flipped open the lid and peered inside.

Empty.

"What the hell is this?" she bristled, a hint of controlled panic edging through her cold façade. "Where is everything?"

"Gone," he said simply, studying her reaction. "I admit to being slightly fla—" He stopped himself, snapping his mouth closed and giving a quick shake of his head. "No. That's wrong. I was actually *completely* flabbergasted when I discovered what was inside."

She glared at him. When she spoke again a moment later, the ice in her voice did nothing whatsoever to hide her panic. "I'll pay you. What do you want?"

"Me?" he asked, his voice taut. "Nothing. Right about now, though, you should probably be more worried about yourself."

"Oh…I see," she said carefully, an all-consuming fear ratcheting her breathing up several notices. "Well, I actually have to go now. I have another appointment." She stood up quickly. Clutching her purse to her chest, she made for the door.

Gas had stood up in the same moment and adroitly stepped in front of her, blocking her passage. "Don't you want to hear the full story, Ms. Wyler?" His voice sounded somewhat brittle to his own ears. "First off, I didn't break into your employer's house. Not my style. I simply dropped by, spur of the moment like, and rang the bell—"

"You did what?!" she shrieked.

"I rang the bell," Gas repeated indifferently. "Spoke with him directly. Jeremy Marsh, right? Very personable. Charismatic even. Can totally understand him being in politics. Anyway, I explained who I was, and he seemed quite shocked when I mentioned your name and told him that you were my client. He hadn't seen or heard from you since you disappeared. Said you left everything of yours behind. You were right on one point, though. He *was* very angry, but not for the reason you said."

Crossing his arms over his chest, he continued. "He explained that you had been his daughters' nanny, and that quite by chance, he'd come home early one day to pick up some papers and found his two little daughters there. All alone. They were only six and eight years old. He instantly called your cell, and when he got no answer, left a scathing message, firing you, effective immediately. It also stated that the locks would be changed and asked you for an address to which your belongings could be sent."

Taking a deep breath, he frowned in feigned confusion. "Oddly, he never heard anything back from you at all. Then he learned from neighbours that you would often frequent a local casino, though of course, usually only when the girls were at school—"

"Let me out of here!" she yelled, trying to push by him.

"By all means," he said affably, stepping aside.

Bolting for the door, she swung it open, and then froze, gasping at the sight of the two uniformed officers standing there. Waiting.

"Oh, and one last thing, Ms. Wyler," Gas called flippantly after her. "Am I right in assuming that I won't be getting paid for retrieving your hatbox?"

She never turned around, but he saw her shoulders flinch slightly before finally slumping as she allowed herself to be led down the corridor, where she and the officers disappeared down the stairs.

Gas stood there, listening to their retreating footsteps until silence returned, frowning sadly and slowly shaking his head.

∗   ∗   ∗

HIS FIRST WIFE WAS INCREDULOUS when he spoke to her next. "News reports are saying that hatbox was full of passports and foreign currency! I can't *believe* it! Is she a con artist? A forger? What?"

Gas shrugged. There wasn't much he could add regarding an active police investigation. He had learned, though, that the box had contained a number of legal passports, most belonging to missing tourists and cruise-ship passengers. A dark tale of an elaborate human-trafficking ring was slowly emerging, and Gwen Wyler's role in the sinister drama was still under investigation.

"I can't say I'm really surprised by the end result," Bella continued after a long moment, her voice almost breezy now. "Everything you told me earlier made it too bizarre to believe that it was really full of simple knick-knacks. Pity about you not being paid the thousand dollars though." She smiled sympathetically. "Bring the drinks and glasses, would you please?" She gathered up cake and candles, and then headed towards the screen door that opened to the back garden.

Picking up the tray as instructed, he called her name to make her stop, but then paused, uncertain what he wanted to say. She glanced back at him expectantly.

"Yes?"

"You simply are the best. You know that, right, Bella?" He sighed. "How in the hell did I ever let you get away?" he lamented sadly, feeling the poignant tug of loss.

Within a wise and knowing look, she quietly said, "I think it had something to do with you meeting wife number two." Then she continued outdoors towards the happy sounds of family chatter and laughter.

Watching her go, Gas caught a glance of his own reflection in the glass portion of the back door and couldn't help but scowl at himself.

"Stupid bastard."

Cleopatra and the Duke

KEITH'S HEART HAMMERED IN ALARM as the reflected glare of headlights seared into his eyes through his semi's side mirror. If he hadn't been squinting so fiercely, his eyes would have widened in surprise.

Where the hell did you come from?!

The dazzle fluttered from behind then as the car steered into the passing lane. For a few short seconds, it ran sleekly alongside him, its yellowed beams etching a pathway over the snow-covered highway. Through the side window's smeared glass, Keith caught a glimpse of its hood ornament: an ornate chrome cat—or rather, a jaguar—seemingly straining against the whipping snow and wind. Then just as quickly, and with a tremendous burst of speed, the Jag slipped back into the driving lane, mere inches in front of his semi's bumper.

"Are you nuts?!" Keith roared, slamming on the brakes and wincing at their loud, hissing protests. Ramming one hand against the horn, its muffled retort echoed in his ears. He tried to read the Jag's plate, but it was well veiled beneath a crust of sloppy snow. With another burst of speed, the Jag spurted insolently ahead, spitting a swath of sludge behind it.

"Stupid ass," muttered Keith, then soon forgot about the car as the wind's velocity intensified. The trailer rocking behind him kept his attention fully on the road. His grip tightened around the wheel. He stared into the inkiness beyond the headlights as the truck's wipers dragged themselves relentlessly across the windscreen. Ice residue built up on the blades as the temperature outside dropped.

Keith cursed softly, straining to see through the streaked glass. "Son of a..." He risked a swift glance to the truck's digital clock and saw that it was only 6:19 p.m. Seemed later. For two hours, he'd been battling the elements as heavy rain had come down, only to have the falling temperatures quickly turn it to sleet, and then to wet, heavy snow. The two hours since it had started now felt like four. Keith released a pent-up breath. Easing his foot from the gas, he geared down.

I should have pulled over at the last rest stop, he thought, berating himself, his brow creasing heavily. Instead, he had changed his mind at the last minute, deciding to push through. He'd hoped the weather forecasters were wrong, but for once, they hadn't been. Slowing still further, he shifted in his seat and leaned forward in an attempt to see more clearly by the dim and jaundiced light of the old truck's high beams, which poked only feeble holes in the mushy deluge.

* * *

ANOTHER HALF HOUR OR SO later, the truck's GPS signaled that Gasoline Alley was just ahead, and then he saw the muted smattering of lights from the plethora of gas stations, cafés, and hotels. The knotted tension in his shoulders slowly oozed away.

With the semi's right turn signal winking its ruby eye, Keith smoothly eased the vehicle down the access corridor, searching for any recognizable rigs. He saw none, but there was one familiar sight: the Jag. Unconsciously, he turned into the same parking area, the truck's chrome shimmering a meteoric display as it glided beneath the saffron streetlamps.

Turning off the ignition and stepping out, Keith quickly slipped a worn slicker over his head, strapped the hood tightly under his chin, and yanked the cord tight. Though he yearned to sprint towards the anticipated warmth of the café's beckoning lights, he scooted head down around the truck and checked everything first. Unlocking the back, he peered inside. Nothing seemed disturbed, so Keith finally relaxed. Then a sudden snow gust snatched the door from his grip. After a brief tussle with it, he ensured that everything was locked and secure, then darted across the lot and through the doorway of the Royal. A tantalizing aroma of strong fresh coffee seared his nostrils.

Removing the dripping slicker, he dropped it carelessly atop a coat stand in the foyer and started sauntering towards the café counter/bar area. The place seemed nice. He usually stopped a little further up the strip when he was in the area, but he approved of what he saw in his initial glances. Antique lamps hung down from the ceiling's wooden beams, their burnished lighting warming the brown-tweed seats and patterned flooring. It all felt very "comfy."

Slouching somewhat, he folded his impressive height into the first available booth he came to, noticing the heads of two people sitting in the next one, ahead of his.

"Coffee?" asked a nasal voice then. Nodding, Keith glanced up into a pair of black-rimmed, blue-shadowed eyes. Orange-slashed lips parted dimly in what Keith took to be a smile. Of sorts, at least.

The woman was expertly juggling a pot of java, a cup, and a saucer in her left hand, and two plates in the right—one with a burger and fries and the other with a salad. With a quick maneuver, she set the cup onto its saucer and poured, paying little attention to the portion that sloshed over the rim. Drawing a menu card from her apron pocket, she then plopped that down onto his table and headed on to the next booth, swaying slightly, though her stiffly sprayed platinum curls remained totally motionless.

The plates she'd been carrying met the table with a definite clatter, and then she wandered in the direction of the sole occupant sitting on a tall stool at the counter. From the next booth over, a feminine voice caught his attention then, speaking passionately: "I'm telling you, Leo, for the last time now. Enough is enough. I don't want to hear that anymore."

"I can say whatever the hell I damn well want!"

Keith could sense almost crushing anger behind Leo's words.

"You know what I mean," the woman said with a hiss, and then lowered her voice and pleaded with him to do the same.

"I'm running this show! Not you!" Leo said, his voice raising an octave (as well as a decibel or two). "And so, I'll talk any which way I please! You just remember your place, little lady!"

Her muffled reply was stifled by a whoop from the bar-stool patron as he yelled "SCORE!" to no one in particular.

Keith turned his head, glancing at the TV screen above the counter, and smiled when he saw the familiar orange and blue uniforms. *Yup,* he thought, shaking his head. *Good thing too, they've been having a tough season so far.*

He turned his gaze back to the heads bobbing in the booth in front of him, with the woman's shoulder-length hair a glossy black, and the man's a short crew. As if realizing they had an audience, the volume and cadence of their words lowered until all Keith could make out was a hum. He finally sighed and closed his eyes.

I'm beat, he thought, sagging further in his seat. *How many hours driving today?* He started calculating in his head. Then he rechecked his work. *Yep. Fourteen. Too damn many.* He sighed again as hunger pangs prodded at him. Opening his eyes, he signaled for the waitress.

"How can you say things like that!" This from the woman in the next booth again.

Keith's head started to pound by the time the waitress returned, pad and pencil in hand. Taking only a cursory glimpse at the menu, he said simply, "I'll take the cutlets and mashed potatoes. Gravy on the side. Hold the salad."

"Sure. Anything else to drink?" she asked, her speech somewhat slurred. Keith decided that she either had a cold or a wad of gum, and then confirmed it to be the latter when he heard it shift in her mouth.

"Maybe a beer," he said, before realizing that this would only worsen his growing headache. "On second thought, make that another coffee. Oh, and can you tell me where the men's room is?"

Her head rotated slightly, nodded in that direction, and then she strolled away. Keith stood up. Walking past the next booth, he noticed the absence of the angry fellow. *Leo,* he remembered from their clashing. A quick glance at the woman, and Keith decided that he liked what he saw. *Man, she's beautiful,* he thought fleetingly. Probably mid-twenties, but nowadays you never knew, did you? That Cleopatra cut suits her perfectly with that dark hair. Her lips trembled slightly as she caught his look, a worried frown creasing her brow, so he quickly continued on his way.

✳ ✳ ✳

ALONE IN THE JOHN, KEITH drenched his face and the back of his neck with cold splashes. Shivering, he risked a look at his reflection in the silvered glass. *You look old, man,* he silently told the weary face.

The face seemed to say, *"Hell, forty-something ain't old."*

Keith shook his aching head. *Maybe not,* he answered just as silently, *but on you, it don't look great. Too many long nights and never enough catch-up time in between for sleep or decent meals.* He decided abruptly to give up coffee. *Even a few cups and I start getting the shakes.*

Taking a deep breath, he paid particular attention to the cratered lines weathering the corners of his mouth and eyes. *Too old for this kind of life, driving all over the country. Never wanted to do it so long. Just seemed like nothing better ever came along.* He attempted a smile but still looking at his reflection, he realized that he couldn't quite pull it off. *Yeah,* he thought as he pulled open the door and started wandering back to his seat. *Too damn old.*

He noticed Leo's side of the bench was still empty and absently wondered where he could have gone. He risked another look at Cleopatra, but saw only the back of her head, her attention seeming to be riveted on some distant spot outside.

Sliding back into his own booth, a sudden spray of headlights through the glass caught Keith's attention. A car was spinning around the slippery parkway, heading down the access road. The streetlamps caught a Jaguar's sleek curves. Keith's eyes narrowed. Not exactly a common sight. *No doubt about it,* he mused. *That has to be the same idiot that passed me earlier.*

He shook his head as the twin cherry taillights blinked out of sight. *Damn fool,* he thought. *Should have stayed put. Crazy to keep driving on a night like this.*

"Excuse me?"

Cleopatra had spoken, her head turning towards him. Keith looked around. No one else was within earshot. The waitress was in the kitchen, and the occupant of the bar stool was leaning excitedly forward, the televised hockey game his sole focus.

"Are you talking to me?" asked Keith finally, raising his voice just enough to be heard.

She laughed. "Yes, I am. I wondered..." She fell silent for a moment, then tried again. "I wondered if I might ask a favour?"

"Depends," Keith replied hesitantly. He was always leery of anyone asking favours. Been burned too many times.

"I was wondering how far you'll be driving tonight?"

He laughed. "Tonight? Are you crazy, lady?" Realizing that this wasn't exactly the most-polite response, he offered her a quick, apologetic smile. "Sorry. No offence. It's just that no one would intentionally keep driving on a night like this."

"Are the roads that bad then?" she asked, sounding concerned. Keith found himself somewhat distracted by the sleekness of her dark tresses. Though normally partial to redheads, he found himself staring just the same.

"Well," he said, "by the look of things, the only fool on the roads tonight is that person who just pulled out. It's really best not to mess around when it's snowing and blowing like it is." *Good advice*, he thought. Though it was not advice he often followed himself.

"Oh."

Silence fell between them then, and after an awkward thirty seconds or so, speaking in a voice that came out far more harshly than he'd intended, he asked her, "So, what's the favour?"

"It's alright. Never mind." She paused briefly, then continued. "Do you know if there's a bus that comes by on a regular schedule?"

"Probably," Keith answered, his irritation mounting, though he suspected much of it was stemming simply from his aching head. *What the hell do I know about buses?* He suddenly felt absolutely famished and wondered what was taking the cutlets so long. Trying to suppress his sour mood, he shrugged and added, "I suppose that waitress might know. Or then again, maybe not. She seems to have enough trouble chewing gum and serving at the same time." He hoped his playful grin would carry the intended humour.

She had just given Keith a small smile in return when it occurred to him that her dining companion, Leo, had been gone an awfully long time. "By the way, where's your friend?"

"He's no friend," she said in a tone both bitter and resigned. "The car that just left? Well, that was him."

"What do you mean? He just *left* you here?"

"Yeah, I guess you could say that." After another small pause, she weakly added, "I just realized what a total jerk he actually is."

Keith was silent. He knew he wasn't the most perfect human being. Hell, he had to be reminded to have a shower or put on a clean shirt before going out to dinner. But one thing he'd never done was leave a lady stranded. Not even when she might have deserved it!

"You need a ride? Is that it? The favour, I mean?"

"Yes," she replied feebly.

"Okay," he said slowly, thinking it through. "Well, maybe… Where do you need to go?" He didn't really want to do this, but hell…leaving her there would probably feel even worse.

"Not far. Just Airdrie."

Airdrie? Keith thought, breathing a sigh of relief. That was just down the road. He could handle that.

"Okay then," he said. "I don't usually take passengers, but I guess I can make an exception this one time. I'm not leaving till morning though. Early. Of course, that's dependant on the weather and the state of the highway. Does that work for you?"

"Sure. Sounds great. Thank you. I'm Cindy, by the way."

"Keith."

"Nice to meet you, Keith." A moment later, she hesitantly added, "There is *one* other thing."

Isn't there always? he thought, on full alert now. "Yeah? What's that?"

"I have a dog with me."

"A dog?" he repeated in disbelief. *Christ, what next?* "So you're stranded here with a dog?"

"His name is Duke. He's very good and won't be any trouble. I promise," she added quickly.

Keith's thoughts raced. *What are you getting yourself into?* He shook his head then, annoyed with himself. *Why are you complaining? Hell, it's only an hour. If that.*

"So where is this dog, anyway? This Duke." He could hardly envision anyone leaving an animal outside on a night like this.

"He's here. Under the table."

"What?" He couldn't believe this. "There are health regulations against that sort of thing!"

"I know," she said simply.

"Are you always like this?" he asked.

"Like what?"

He sighed. "You don't say much, do you?"

"Only once I get to know someone. So, I can pay you if that helps. But do we have a deal?"

"Don't worry about paying. I'm driving right past Airdrie as it is. It's the dog thing I'm thinking about. Listen, can we talk in a minute? I'm just going to go see what's keeping my food." He'd just stood up when a question occurred to him. "How'd you get him in here, anyway? The dog, I mean."

She laughed. "I think I might have told the waitress he was my support animal."

"Uh-huh. And she fell for that, did she?" Keith found this hard to swallow. Cleopatra certainly didn't look like she had any health issues, but of course, you never know.

"No, she didn't believe a word. And he's not, by the way. A support animal. She said I could keep him inside anyway as long as I kept him out of sight. If the owner knew, she'd lose her job, but luckily he's not here tonight."

Keith walked over to her booth, and leaning over, he took a quick glance under the table, expecting to find some kind of fluffy, mindless poodle. The dog that lifted its head at his intrusion, however, had intelligent eyes that were now on full alert and fixated on Keith's face.

"Goddamn! That's a German Shepherd and damn near as big as a horse! Looks like he could take my head off if he wanted to."

"Maybe," she said evasively. "Would you like to join me? We could go over the logistics for tomorrow."

"Sure," Keith replied, a bit hesitantly. "About the dog though… He's safe, isn't he?"

She laughed, her eyes actually sparkling. "Just a big baby, really. Wouldn't hurt a fly."

"It's not the fly I'm worried about," he answered, sitting down and forgetting all about pestering the waitress.

His food arrived about a minute later, accompanied by a bowl of water for Duke. "Sorry it took so long," the waitress said. "Short staffed. I brought a bowl of water for the dog. I got one at home too," she confessed, sounding a bit flustered, "I could bring him some leftovers too if you think he's hungry." She looked at Cindy for approval.

"He's fine," Cindy answered sharply. "He doesn't eat scraps."

"Okay," the woman answered stiffly.

Keith sensed the friction between them and wondered what it was all about. He opened his mouth to ask exactly that when the outer door suddenly opened and a crush of voices suddenly filled the silence. Keith managed to make out just a smattering of their excited babble. Something about a big accident and the southbound lanes being closed.

The waitress abruptly hustled off to deal with the incoming fray.

✳ ✳ ✳

A SHORT WHILE LATER, AS Keith finished polishing off his so-so cutlets, he looked at Cleopatra—*Cindy,* he reminded himself. "Listen, Cindy, I've got to get some shut-eye. I'll be checking road and weather conditions before we head out, but I'd like to be on the road by six."

"Six? That's pretty darn early," Cindy complained. "Can't you make it a bit later?"

"I got to be somewhere." *Favours,* he thought tiredly. *People who ask for them always push for more.* He vowed not to fall for it this time. "Six," he said again, and gave her a look that told her not to push any further. "I noticed there's a motel next door. You better get yourself a room before everything fills up. It looks like it's going to be a busy night everywhere."

"Uh…Actually, I already got a room," she said quickly. "Well, Leo did. I got a key, but…" She let her voice trail off as her eyes lowered.

"But what, Cindy?" Keith was suddenly exhausted, and his good Samaritan gesture was quickly turning into a grind.

"Well, it's just that they won't allow the dog. So, yeah, I have a room. But Duke doesn't." She started fidgeting with her cup. "Is there any way you could take him? In your truck? I mean, it *is* a sleeper unit, right?"

"How do you know my truck?" Keith asked brusquely, sudden misgivings about the whole arrangement crowding his thoughts.

"I saw you get out of it when you got here," she said defensively, a stony stare accompanying her words.

"Sorry," he said quickly. "Didn't mean to imply anything." He was starting to feel like a bit of an ass. "I don't think that Duke here is going to be interested in going off with me. After all, he's your dog and—"

"Look, there isn't any other choice, is there? I can't take him with me. So if you don't, I'm going to have to leave him tied up outside."

Keith involuntarily glanced through the window at the blowing snow. *Damn it all to hell!* With a heavy sigh, he gave in. "Okay, okay, I'll take him. Assuming he'll let me, anyway."

"Of course he'll let you," she said, her tone softening once more. "He's just a big baby. Come here, Duke," she said cajolingly, looking under the table. "Come on…"

With that, the giant dog emerged and stood quietly beside the table, splitting doleful looks between Cindy and Keith. His sudden appearance drew some glances and a bit of chatter from the other people now seated around them.

"Okay," Keith said as he took the leash. "Come on, J.W. Let's see what you're really like."

"J.W.?" Cindy repeated warily. "What's that about?"

Keith shrugged. "John Wayne." When there was no look of recognition on her face, he raised his eyebrows and elaborated. "You know…the *original* Duke?"

Cindy didn't bite, her perplexed look threatening to become a permanent fixture.

Keith shook his head. "Doesn't matter. I'll explain tomorrow. Six a.m. Got it?"

"No problem," she replied airily.

"Okay, Duke, it's just you and me, guy, so we gotta make this work. Let's go." With that, Keith turned and headed back out towards the door.

"Seeing eye dog," Keith muttered in response to the stunned looks he received from those he passed. "Helping me find my truck." He laughed at the notion and smiled when a few chuckles followed him to the doorway.

Duke stood silently as Keith went to the young guy at the cash desk and paid his tab. At the last moment, and for no particular reason, he added a generous tip. "This is for the waitress. Um…I didn't catch her name." He looked around, but the woman was nowhere in sight.

"Marion?" the guy answered somewhat distractedly, already dismissing Keith as he worked to wrangle his cell phone from his back pocket with one hand.

"Marion," Keith repeated. "Okay, thanks."

Pulling on his slicker, he and Duke ran towards the truck.

✳ ✳ ✳

A FIVE-A.M. CHECK ON THE weather and road conditions convinced Keith that there would be no need to delay his day's travel. The snowfall had lessened somewhat but hadn't stopped completely yet. It didn't really matter to him though because the southbound lanes had been cleared and reopened. That was all he'd really needed to know. Zipping his jacket, he stepped out from the cab of his truck and hurried back towards the Royal. When he reached it, he stomped heavy snow from his boots, then opened the door and savoured the café's warmth for a moment.

"Where the hell is the dog?!"

Stunned by the intensity of this sudden question that had come out of nowhere so early in the morning, Keith let the café door clunk noisily shut behind him. *"Excuse* me?" he offered, just barely awake and craving a coffee.

"The dog?" the shrill voice asked again. "Remember him?!"

Getting truly annoyed now, Keith struggled to dredge up the name of the voice's owner. *Was it Marion?*

"Listen, Marion—it *is* Marion, right?" She nodded, so he pressed on. "It's *so* nice to *meet* you, Marion," he replied caustically, striding towards her with a scowl. "I'm Keith, by the way, and the dog is just fine, thank you very much. He's in the truck, looking for his breakfast—same as me, in case you're interested." He was pissed off now. "Oh, right," he added with a snap of his fingers, "good morning to you too. Now…What's with the goddamn attitude?"

Marion raced from behind the counter where she'd been standing and over to the glass door, staring out into the winter-morning darkness beyond at the interior of his semi's cab, illuminated clearly by nearby streetlights. The shadowed outline of a canine sentinel was clearly evident inside, sitting bolt upright on the passenger seat.

"Sorry, sorry, sorry…" Marion stammered, completely flustered now as she took a deep breath and worked to calm herself down.

"What's going on?" he asked, taking a breath and glancing around. "All I'm looking for is a coffee and something to eat. Oh, and if you've got some of those scraps for the dog, that would be great too. I'm sure he's pretty hungry. And can you tell me if you've seen that girl from last night come in yet? Cindy? I'm supposed to drop her and her mutt off in Airdrie this morning."

Marion took another deep breath, held it for a moment, and then released it in a huff before finally looking him in the eye. "Gone," she said flatly. "Left last night right after you did. Some guy in a Jag picked her up."

"What?" He shook his head, not believing his ears. "No, you got it wrong. That guy left way earlier." His mind was reeling as he tried to process this. "I'm…I'm supposed to be giving her a ride to…" His mouth opened and closed a few more times, with no words emerging. Finally, he found his voice. "Well, she *can't* just be *gone!* You got that wrong somehow," he repeated, inanely.

"Oh, really?" Marion said sarcastically before working to dial her tone back to something approaching civility. "And yet, the fact remains that she isn't here." She looked at him for a response, but he was too stunned to give her one.

She shook her head at him. "I bet she didn't tell you *everything* about that dog either, did she? That she was trying to get rid of him? When she and her friend first got here, she was leashing him up outside with a sign around his neck that said, 'Free dog.' She tell you that part? If you don't believe me, I can show you the sign. I've still got it."

Keith was stunned. "Crap." He wanted to say something more, but nothing came to mind. Finally, he frowned. "I thought the highway was closed last night. So how did she leave?"

"Northbound was open."

His thoughts were whirling. *Face it, ya stupid sap... You got played and never even saw it coming.*

"Keith," Marion said, her tone softer now, "if it makes you feel any better, I've met a lot of Cindy types. A person does in a job like this. You're probably not the first person she's scammed, and you won't be the last either. If it helps at all, she was initially just going to dump the dog on the side of the road. Can you believe that! With the weather and all, though, her fella wouldn't let her."

Keith finally came to his senses and looked at her sharply with suspicion. "And how do *you* know all this?"

Marion smiled wryly. "When people think you're invisible, they tend to talk too much." She shrugged. "I could see her roping you in and wasn't too surprised when I saw her pull out later without the dog. I just didn't know what she'd done with him. I checked outside, but he wasn't tied up. Kind of had it figured that she'd pawned him off on you, but I didn't know which truck was yours. A few more semis had pulled in by then, and it was already pretty full. Anyway, when my shift ended at two, the southbound was still closed, and since I couldn't go home anyway and had heard you say that you were leaving at six, I just wanted to make sure the dog was okay, and that you had him."

Keith turned and stared back outside for a long moment. "When he and I got to the truck last night," he said quietly, "I let him up into the passenger seat, and then went around to the driver's side, opened the door, and pulled out the snow brush from under the seat. When I leaned his way, planning to sweep away the snow that had gotten on the seat around him, he cowered...actually crouched right down on all fours to try and make himself smaller and started whimpering like—" His voice caught in his throat for a second. "Like I was going to hurt him."

He paused then and turned to look at her. "Do you think someone was? Hurting him, I mean? Beating him?" The question hung in the air between them briefly before she slowly nodded.

"Yeah," she answered sadly. "Yeah, I think so. Maybe…Something sure didn't feel right. He was just too damn quiet."

"Yeah." Keith took a shaky breath, and then clearing his throat, he wiped a fist roughly across his eyes. When he turned back to look at Marion, his eyes were bright beneath his furrowed brow. "Do you think I could bring him in for just a minute? Maybe give him a drink and something to eat?"

"No problem. I kept those leftovers from last night just in case." After a moment, she softly asked, "What are you going to do with him?"

Keith inhaled sharply at the question, and then turned back once more to stare morosely outside, deep in thought. "Damned if I know."

She chuckled quietly at this, and he suddenly realised that he was fighting a battle that had already been lost. "Bloody hell."

Stepping back from the door, he turned around again to look at her straight on with a resigned stare. "Well, I guess I know at least one dumb-ass trucker who might have room for a sharp-looking dude to ride sidekick with him. You know…The type of partner who'll let him do all the talking and complaining and just agree with everything he says?"

"Yeah, I'm guessing you probably do," she said approvingly. Pulling out a menu card then, she said lightly, "So how about you go get your dog now, and we'll see what he has to say about that arrangement? If you remember, the original Duke wasn't exactly willing to ride shotgun with just anyone." She smiled softly at him.

Keith returned her smile. "Yeah, you may be right. I could easily end up being the sidekick, with Duke calling all the shots."

"Entirely possible," she answered with a huge smile.

* * *

AS KEITH HEADED BACK OUTSIDE towards the truck, he found himself grinning at first, and then laughing as he watched his new road companion jumping excitedly back and forth between the front seats of his semi, probably scratching the shit out of them.

Shaking his head at Duke's antics, he picked up the pace. It was still cold and unpleasant, but he found that he didn't really mind.

Screw the weather forecast...I think it's going to be a damn fine day.

Printed in the USA
CPSIA information can be obtained
at www.ICGtesting.com
JSHW040459240424
61759JS00014B/204

9 781038 303981